Hazel's Phantasmagoria

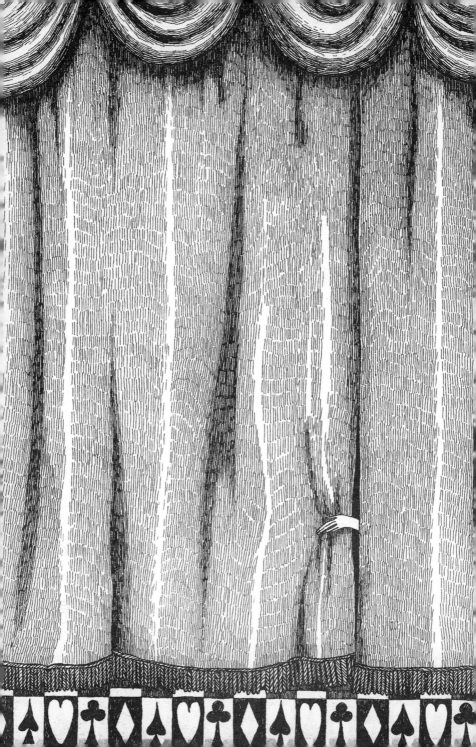

Hazel's
Phantasmagoria

LEANDER DEENY

Quercus

First published in Great Britain in 2008 by
Quercus
21 Bloomsbury Square
London
WC1A 2NS

A CIP catalogue reference for this book is available
from the British Library

ISBN (HB) 978 1 84724 423 9
ISBN (TPB) 978 1 84724 424 6

10 9 8 7 6 5 4 3 2 1

Designed and typeset by Rook Books, London
Printed and bound in England by Clays Ltd, St Ives plc.

For Camille and Isabel

Good evening

Your mother probably deserves to die.

Yes, I understand – you love your mummy. But how well do you really know her? You've only known her as long as you've been alive - and she was around for years before that. Think about it – years! I'll bet you a hundred pounds that in those long, lonely, boring years before you were born, she did some things she hasn't told you about.

Look into her eyes, and see how she reacts if you say the following words:

Gossip!
Manipulation!
Bullying!
Deceit!
Embezzlement!
Arson!
Fraud!
Burglary!
Cattle-rustling!
Devil-worship!

Try shouting them out at random during dinner. How does she react? Does she look embarrassed? Does she look like she's trying to cover something up? I bet she's got a funny expression on her face. That expression, of course, is guilt.

Oh! You don't believe your mother could possibly be guilty of cattle-rustling? Well – that only goes to show how naïve you are. But I'm sure by the time you reach your mother's age you'll be guilty of the most terrible lies, betrayals, and animal-abductions. Everybody does it!

So. Even though you love your mummy, she, like most people older than you, is ripe for extermination.

Oh, do stop crying.

Now, whoever is going to be responsible for killing your mother is going to have a difficult task ahead of them. Murder is a serious business. It takes months of planning. It requires special equipment. It is highly illegal.

Most importantly, once you've done it, you can't ever take it back. I am sorry to say that it is not much fun being a murderer. There's the mess for a start – burying a body in the middle of the night is both mucky and tiring. Then there's getting arrested – which usually involves the police twisting your arm and bumping your head on the door of the police car. Then there's being put on trial – which involves answering difficult questions and being called lots of horrible names. Then, finally, there's going to jail – which is pretty much the worst place in the world.

So, even though your mother deserves to die, the downsides to killing her are enormous.

But, enormous though those downsides are, they are not enough to deter everybody. Because lots of people kill people. They have done it throughout the history of the world. They do it every day.

This is a book about why.

Eugenia, Lady Pequierde

The First Chapter of this Book

They were only halfway through the drive, and Hazel was already furious.

'But I don't want to stay with *them*. I want to come with *you. I like you.*'

'You like them as well, dear,' said her mother.

'I do NOT. What was the last thing I said about them?'

Hazel's mother sighed.

'You said – oh dear, let me get this right – you said that staying with them would be worse than staying in a wasps' nest. Even if you had to cook and clean for the wasps, or something like that. Then you said that even if none of the wasps volunteered to organise the wasp parade, and you had to organise it all by yourself, and you had to make little paper hats for the wasps, and a little mermaid costume for one of the wasps to ride on an ocean-themed float – I mean by this point I'd already got the message, you didn't need to go on, but of course you did – something about

3

inventing a holiday for the wasp parade to be celebrating, because wasps don't have holidays, but they do want parades, and they don't think about things like that when asking little girls to organise parades for their stupid non-existent holidays. You were bright red by this point. Even then, you said you would still rather stay with the wasps than stay with Aunt Eugenia and cousin Isambard.'

'Exactly. Does that *sound* like the sort of thing I would say if I liked Aunt Eugenia and cousin Isambard?'

' . . . No.'

Hazel folded her arms and glared triumphantly out of the car window. Then she looked a little puzzled.

'Did I really say all that stuff about the wasp parade?'

Hazel's father, who hadn't said anything for hours, and had just been watching the road, spoke finally.

'You'd had rather a lot of sugar that day, sweetheart, and I don't think you were in your right mind. Not unlike today, in fact. How many Insanity Bars have you eaten?'

'Never you mind how many Insanity Bars I've eaten. I can be in a bad mood without eating sugar, thank you very much. Maybe I'm just *angry* with you.'

Hazel's father sighed.

'I do hope the government bans those Insanity Bars one of these days. Apparently they have eighty-six teaspoons of sugar in each bar.'

'That's impossible, Dad.'

'Eighty-six teaspoons of sugar! That's enough to make a horse . . . to make a horse . . . well, whatever sugar does to a horse, I'm sure eighty-six teaspoons would do an awful lot of it.'

4

'I'm not a horse, *Dad.*'

'Sometimes I wish you were. It would save a fortune on Insanity Bars.'

Hazel stuck out her tongue and rammed her fingers in her ears.

* * *

Hazel had been against the whole thing from the start. Mum and Dad had told her they were going to Egypt for three weeks, but at first that was all they said. Then, halfway through the summer term, they finally owned up to the fact that they were going on their own. Hazel would not be coming with them. When she asked why, her father simply replied, 'Egypt is a dangerous country – I am not having my only child eaten by a camel, buried in a sand dune, or squashed by a falling pyramid.' No other explanation was offered.

The drive down to Aunt Eugenia's house took four hours, and Hazel passed in and out of sleep, sitting amidst heaps of books and chocolate wrappers like a sleepy gerbil in a bundle of straw. They would stop there for dinner, and Mum and Dad would drive on to catch a late plane from Heathrow.

And then the two weeks would begin.

Hazel played I spy with her mother, and listened to stories on the car CD player, and they stopped at a service station to get coffee for Dad, magazines for Mum, and chocolates for Hazel (Mum and Dad were being unusually free with the chocolates that day).

The countryside around Aunt Eugenia's house was stupid.

Well, that's not fair — it was probably rolling, or flat, or covered in ancient rocks or something, but Hazel was in such a bad mood that she did not even feel like *looking* at the countryside, let alone describing it in a clever way.

So the countryside was stupid.

Hazel hated her Aunt Eugenia. She hardly ever saw her, and whenever she did it was horrid. She remembered the last time she had met her, at Christmas three years ago. Mum and Dad had spent three full days decorating the house, cooking the turkey, and wrapping the presents, but Eugenia didn't turn up on time. As they waited for her arrival, the sprouts all went cold, the cat ate the Christmas pudding, and Hazel got so annoyed waiting for her presents that she buried the TV remote control in the flowerbed.

Finally Eugenia turned up, and while Mum and Dad did their best to be polite and pretend nothing was wrong, Eugenia proceeded to be as rude as possible for the whole meal.

'Who on earth are you?' Eugenia had said to Hazel, apparently having never taken any interest in her niece whatsoever.

'I'm Hazie,' Hazel had said, Hazie being her baby name, which she had DEFINITELY grown out of since then.

Hazel's mother interjected.

'Hazel, dear, say Hazel.'

Eugenia continued her inquisition.

'Well, how old are you, child?'

'I'm theven.' She'd definitely grown out of saying theven, as well. Definitely.

'How ridiculous,' snorted Eugenia, obviously unimpressed. 'Isambard is also seven years old, and I can tell just by looking at the two of you that he's twice as clever as you are. He's phenomenally clever for his age, and has already learned things you could not possibly imagine. Isn't that right, Isambard?'

In response, Isambard said simply, 'Bogota is the capital of Colombia,' and looked glumly at the floor.

'Very good, dear. Do *you* know the capital of Colombia, child?'

Hazel had thought this a strange question, as Isambard had just told her what the capital of Colombia was.

'Bogota?' she ventured.

Eugenia seemed confused.

'Well . . . yes, yes it is. I see you know some things. But other than that I'm sure you're quite hopelessly stupid.'

Hazel had looked to her parents for help, but they had deserted her to improvise some kind of pudding in the kitchen.

'Mexico City is the capital of Mexico,' Isambard had said, still staring at the floor. This hadn't seemed as impressive as the last one.

'Child, do you have many friends? I have always thought that stupid people should at least be good at making friends. It is a skill I somehow never got the hang of.'

Hazel had, at this point, begun to cry. Making friends was perhaps the very thing she was worst at in the world. Thus far she had a grand total of zero.

'Oh, do stop blubbering, child.' At this point Eugenia had knelt down, very awkwardly, to look Hazel in the eye.

'No matter what happens, no matter how sad or lonely you are, no matter how much you want to break down into tears, you must never, ever let anyone see you cry.' Eugenia had rubbed her tired eyes with her long fingers and stared thoughtfully away. 'Ever. Understand?'

Hazel had nodded, though she had no idea what Eugenia meant. What she had understood was that Aunt Eugenia was one of the meanest people she had ever met, and she wanted to spend as little time with her as possible.

Then Eugenia poked her in the forehead.

'Remember, child! Yes? Remember!'

Isambard shook his head and said nothing.

After Eugenia left, Hazel summed up the courage to tell her mother and father that Aunt Eugenia had poked her. They refused to believe her, and told her to stop telling fibs. Then Dad realised the remote control was missing, Hazel admitted she'd buried it but couldn't remember where, and her parents became far too angry with Hazel to bother about being angry with Eugenia.

In fact, much to Hazel's annoyance, it went down in history as 'The Christmas When Hazel Buried the Remote' rather than 'The Christmas When Mum and Dad found out Aunt Eugenia was a Dangerous Lunatic and Reported to her to the Police, Who Locked her up in Jail Forever to Save Children all Over the World from Being Poked in the Face'.

* * *

The car had begun to smell pretty nice, Hazel thought — what with all the chocolate she had been eating. She'd tired herself out with the shouting, and was drifting off into a nice nap, when Dad dropped a bombshell.

'We're there, everyone!'

Hazel sat bolt upright, and shrieked, 'I can't believe it, three weeks with that *witch!*'

After hours of complaining, this was the final straw — Mum, who had until now been a vision of patience, snapped.

'Hazel! I will *not* have you talking like that about my sister! She's my big sister — my *only* sister, and you may hate her, but I love her, and she has never done *anything* to you!'

Hazel's mother hardly ever got as cross as this. She was a calm woman, and could put up with Hazel's tantrums for hours on end — but she had at last been pushed too far. Her face turned red, and her eyes opened wide, as she welled up with emotions she rarely expressed.

Hazel didn't know what to say.

'But . . .'

' . . . and DON'T start all the nonsense about being poked in the face again! You are my daughter, and I love you, but sometimes you take a dislike to people and just start making up stories about them, young lady, and besides you have *such* a temper on you, and maybe, just *maybe* that's why you've had so much trouble making friends at school!'

Hazel tried to reply, but before she could her throat dried up and shrank to the size of a pea, and she felt tears begin to stream down her face. Mum turned away in a huff, and Hazel was left to think about what she'd done. She wasn't at all used to seeing Mum like this, and right now it was the last thing she needed.

Making little whimpering sounds, she wiped her tear-strewn face, and looked desperately out of the window — as if she might see something there that would allay her mother's fury. Instead, all she saw was the drive up to Eugenia's house.

Aunt Eugenia's house was the sort of house that someone completely appalling might have. It had a ridiculous driveway lined with ghastly trees and covered in ugly gravel. It sat in the middle of twenty acres of pointless land, next to a barn the colour of poo, with a wood behind it that almost certainly smelled of farts, and a lake in front of it that looked like thousands of people had vomited into a big hole.

The building itself had obviously been built by goons, out of the worst stones they could find. It had four rubbish towers, lots of rubbish windows, and a large wooden door big enough for a big idiot to pass through.

The car made annoying crunchy noises all the way up the drive.

It started to rain.

Hazel tried to hold back another flood of tears.

Dad ran out of the car using Mum's magazine to cover his head (you don't take umbrellas to Egypt), and knocked on the door. Obviously there was a big door-knocker shaped like a face, which Hazel was sure was a special birthday present from Satan.

A smaller door in the big door opened up, though Hazel could not see inside it. There didn't seem to be many lights on in the house.

Dad ran back to the car.

'You two run inside – I'll get Hazel's bag out of the boot.'

Hazel took a deep breath, and hurried out of the car, across the driveway, past the two trees in front of the door, up to the door, and into the house.

It had been three years since she had last seen Aunt Eugenia, and now, here she was. Face to face, after all this time.

And what did Aunt Eugenia look like?

Stupid.

The Second
Chapter of
this Book

Eugenia was a widow.

She was the elder sister of Hazel's mother, Katie, and had impressed everyone enormously by marrying a baronet called Sir Podbury Pequierde. The wedding took place on Mount Kilimanjaro, with Podbury and Eugenia taking their vows riding a pair of elephants.

Ever since the day of that lavish wedding she had been impossible. She moved into Podbury's enormous house in the country, with its acres of land, and four towers, and hardly ever visited her sister. She dressed in the finest clothes, ate the most delicious food, and treated everyone like something she found on the bottom of her shoe.

It is perhaps worth mentioning that Hazel's father, Dougal, was a doctor. There were plenty of people at Hazel's school who called Hazel 'posh' (they called her lots of other things as well – like 'plop-head' and 'ding-bat') and Eugenia wasn't really so much better off than her sister Katie. The difference was that Eugenia was Lady Pequierde and Katie was just Katie.

Podbury was a dashing, tall man with jet-black hair and a heroic moustache. He owned a huge mansion in the country. He rode horses, went shooting all over the world, and above all gambled. Gambled like there was no tomorrow. Eventually, of course, there *was* no tomorrow, as he discovered one sunny afternoon when he fell into the tiger enclosure of London Zoo and was torn to pieces.

Since then, Eugenia had been, if anything, ruder. She had been robbed of the man that made her better than other people, and the man who provided her with beautiful clothes and fancy food. She had thought long and hard about who she should take her anger out on, and decided it was probably best if she just took it out on everyone.

Further to losing her husband, she was also not quite as wealthy as she had once been, Podbury having gambled most of their money away. He certainly did love to gamble. He gambled on which party would win an election, and on which film would win an Oscar, and on whether his first child would be a boy or a girl. He gambled on which of his friends would be the first to get married, on which of his friends would be the first to go to jail, and on which of his friends would be the first to be made Pope. Amazingly, one of his friends, Antonio, *was* made Pope, but unfortunately he had bet on Alice.

Podbury always lost the bet. I know what you're thinking. You're thinking, 'Well he must have won some of the bets!'

But you're wrong. He lost, without exception, every bet

he ever made. Which is a thing that can happen, if you're unlucky, and Podbury was *extremely* unlucky. For example, he married Eugenia.

Now, if it had been otherwise – if the Conservatives *had* won the election, or if that film he made starring himself *had* won an Oscar, or if his first child *had* been a bouncing baby girl called Isambardia Pequierde, then there might have been a little more left of the Pequierde family fortune.

Instead, all that was left was a few servants and the house – that horrible house, with horrible Aunt Eugenia in it. Bits of stone were falling off the towers. The lake was filthy. The curtains had started to rot. The windows had developed a rare problem called 'window-plague' which only affects the very dirtiest windows in the world. And there was no money to repair any of it.

So, when Dougal and Katie finished their dinner, and went to the airport, they left their daughter Hazel in a big, scary, collapsing old house with Lady Pequierde, the young Sir Isambard Pequierde, an old butler called Pude, a gardener called Boynce, a cook called Mrs Dungeon, and nobody else for miles around.

* * *

Dinner was over, and Hazel was sitting with Eugenia and Isambard in the drawing room. It was a large, dark room with three great windows that no one ever opened. The carpet was bottle green and covered in stains. The ceiling had cobwebs in its corners. But perhaps most disgustingly, the walls were lined with the heads of animals.

There was a warthog over the door, with four mighty tusks protruding from its jaw. There was a stag on the far wall whose glass eyes had fallen out years ago, making it look even more horrifying than a disembodied head normally does. In between were smaller animals – jackals, and gazelle, and wildcats – all of them covered in dust, moth-eaten and unloved. Finally, above the fireplace hung the most frightful of all – a giraffe. Its long, once-graceful neck was easily six feet long, though it might have been longer when it was still attached to a body. Its gold and brown fur had turned grey from the smoke of the fire, and its glass eyes stared out coldly into nothingness.

Hazel imagined having her head cut off, stuffed, and hung on a wall. It didn't sound very nice. But then she looked over at Aunt Eugenia, remembered she'd be staying here for three weeks, and thought maybe being stuffed wouldn't be quite so bad.

Remembering how angry Mum had been when she left, Hazel was trying her best to swallow her pride and be nice to Eugenia.

'That was a very nice dinner, Auntie.'

Eugenia did not look impressed. She stared at Hazel threateningly, and drank her tea as if Hazel hadn't spoken at all.

Aunt Eugenia never took off her riding boots. They were shiny black boots that went up to her knees, and all the rest of her black clothes looked grey by comparison. She wore a tattered old jumper, and held its sleeves tightly in her hands. She held her shoulders hunched high up by her neck. Her nails had been smartly done with nail-varnish at some point last year, but by now were long and yellow and chipped. She wore black jeans, and her white hair projected diagonally up out of the back of her head like the tail of a comet. She looked as if she never slept. She always had a pained expression on her face, and the only thing that ever seemed to relieve her was being brought a steaming cup of tea by Mrs Dungeon. When one of these cups of tea, in a cracked old mug, met Aunt Eugenia's dried lips, and slipped down her throat, a brief expression of calm would pass across her face, before that look of constant discomfort returned.

'Where do you go to school, child?'

'Ashford Primary,' said Hazel, as cheerfully as she could manage.

Eugenia looked confused, and then annoyed.

'Never heard of it.' She looked out the window and held the mug of tea up to her nose. 'Isambard's just been given a place at a very good school. They're accepting him early, because he's so clever.'

Isambard, for the briefest moment, looked up from the book he was reading. He was a small, pale boy, with sad, brown eyes, and buckets of thick black hair in a curly mess on top of his head. He wore a black suit, a white shirt, shiny brown shoes, and a black bow tie. Seeing that no response was required of him, he returned to his book.

'He's very clever, you know. Are you clever?' said Eugenia.

Hazel sighed. She did think she was clever, but it was hard to get her teachers to agree.

'No, not really,' Hazel laughed and made a funny, happy

face. 'I'm just a silly old dingbat! I'm not clever at all! Ha ha!'

'No. I shouldn't think you are.' Eugenia sighed a deep sigh. 'Oh, God.'

' . . . Um . . . are you all right, Aunt Eugenia?'

Eugenia looked stern.

'Don't ask me if I'm all right. What would you know? How could you possibly understand how I'm feeling?'

'Yes, Aunt Eugenia.'

Isambard continued to read, apparently taking no notice of the conversation.

Eugenia scratched her head with her long nails. She was in a green armchair, with her legs folded beneath her, and brown cushions all around.

'Isambard's revising at the moment, aren't you, Isambard?'

Isambard looked up, nodded sheepishly, and, when Eugenia stopped looking at him, looked away again.

'He's revising. He'll have to work extremely hard to keep up with all the older boys at his special school. So he's revising. That's what it'll be like when you get a little older and go to big school. If the big school lets you in, that is, what with you being so stupid.' She thought for a moment. 'You can't be clever unless you revise. He revises a lot. That's probably why you're not clever – hard work and application.' She went to drink her tea. There was none left. She looked with amazement and fury into her mug, before deciding what to do.

'DUNGEON! *Tea!*'

Hazel jumped, but not as much as the first time. You got used to these outbursts. She was sitting upright on a long yellow sofa. Well, it was long, but only one corner was usable, as red wine stains covered most of it. Mouldy red wine stains that had not been properly cleaned when they first did their staining. Mouldy red wine stains with mushrooms growing out of them.

It was easy for mushrooms to grow in this house, as the old stones were very damp, and Aunt Eugenia never opened the curtains. Dark and wet is what mushrooms like. If you want to live in the dark, say in a cave or a crypt or an ancient pyramid, it's very important to keep it dry, otherwise you get mushrooms. Trust me.

But Eugenia didn't like paying for things like builders, and in fairness to her there wasn't a lot of money left, particularly seeing as she'd been sitting in the same armchair drinking tea for five years, and there's not a lot of jobs where you get to sit in an armchair and drink tea. Truth to tell, most employers are reluctant to hire people to sit in armchairs and drink tea. It's just not economically efficient. Even tea manufacturers who need to test how nice their tea is don't hire people to sit and drink it any more. They just test it on rabbits. Rabbits love a nice cup of tea.

Pude arrived at the door.

'Sorry, ma'am. Mrs Dungeon has gone off to beddy-byes, and I'm serving the tea now.'

'To bed! What? Is she deranged? I need my tea!'

'Yes, ma'am, but it's one in the morning, and Mrs Dungeon isn't getting any younger.'

One in the morning! Hazel's parents had left at seven! How had she managed to spend six hours with these people? She'd spent a good hour on toilet breaks throughout the night, she reckoned, and about an hour's worth of actual conversation. So that left four hours and forty minutes of looking at the mushrooms, worrying about the mushrooms, and wishing very hard that she was somewhere else.

'I do hope I've prepared the tea properly, ma'am. I'll be downstairs if you need me.'

Eugenia glared at Pude and said nothing – but took the tea gratefully.

Pude was like a worried little potato. Hazel had come to like him over the evening, as whatever horrible things Eugenia said to him, he just grinned and took it. He was in his sixties at least, and almost as short as Hazel. His head and body were perfectly round, without any of that silly neck business most people's bodies spend so much time and effort on. He wore a battered tailcoat, with a cheerful yellow bow tie.

'This is disgusting,' said Eugenia.

' Sorry, ma'am. I'll make you another.'

'No! It will only be as vile as this one. Get out of my sight.'

'Yes, ma'am.'

Pude began to go, when Eugenia stopped him.

'Pude!'

'Yes, ma'am?'

'What are you, Pude?'

Pude smiled as if nothing was wrong.

'A nitwit, ma'am.'

'That's right. Now go away.'

Isambard said nothing during all of this.

Seeing he was free to go, Pude waddled off out of the room. Eugenia picked up a framed photograph in front of her. She looked at it with anger and despair, then put it down again, and went back to her tea. Hazel could not see what it was a photo of, but she thought it must be a photo of something Eugenia didn't like very much.

' . . . Well, I think I might need to go to bed, Aunt . . .'

'You pathetic weakling. Bed? *Bed*! You're young – you're full of energy. You should be up late revising like Isambard. You're never going to get anywhere being lazy.'

Hazel felt very upset. What with having no friends and terrible marks in school, she worried a lot about never getting anywhere.

'But I'm really tired . . .'

'Ridiculous! The problem with you . . . with you . . . what's your name? Almond or something, isn't it? Or is it Cashew?'

'Actually it's Hazel. Should I stay up and read?'

'Don't toady to me like that! Stand up for yourself, Cashew.'

Hazel groaned.

'It's Hazel. I thought you wanted me to stay up and revise. Please . . . I'll be good and do whatever you say . . .'

Eugenia looked as if Hazel had betrayed her in some way.

'Oh, you are a *creep*, aren't you. I think you should get off to bed, *now*.'

'I'm sorry! Please, I just want to be friends – maybe I could make your tea for you?'

'If you made my tea for me, I wouldn't be able to drink

it without thinking of you. In fact, it would probably smell of you. Now get off to bed before you make me really angry.'

Why did Eugenia never say any of this when Mum and Dad were around? Mum and Dad would put a stop to it if they heard it. Come to that, why did Isambard just sit there and say nothing whilst his mother behaved so badly? Presumably he agreed with all the crazy things his mother had to say – presumably he was just as bad as she was.

On that thought, Hazel sat up, edged her way around the mushrooms, and darted quickly out the door.

'Good night, Macadamia,' spat Eugenia as the door swung shut.

This was going to be a very long three weeks.

Hazel fumbled her way up the dark staircase. Eugenia wouldn't let any lights be put on in any room that she wasn't currently in, and there were trays of food smashed on the floor where Pude or Dungeon had tripped up in the dark. There were no carpets. Just stone on the ground floor, and damp wood from the first floor up. There were lots of rooms, but most of them weren't inhabited by anything other than mice and spiders. Hazel was grateful to be in a room on the first floor, so she didn't have to walk too far up that dark staircase to go to bed.

What was she going to *do* for three weeks? Other than go mad? She closed the door of her huge, empty room, and folded her clothes on the dark, wooden floor. There were ancient paintings of dead Pequierdes on the walls, and the bed was a giant, sullen mass of rotting wood and faded velvet covers. It looked like a bed that was in a bad mood.

She had already brushed her teeth during one of the numerous trips she took to the toilet, and she couldn't be bothered with washing her face, seeing as Mum wasn't here.

She curled up in a tight ball in her enormous four-poster bed. The sheets smelled horrible, and she drifted off holding her hand over her nose. As she slept, she dreamt of being somewhere else.

The Third Chapter  of this Book

As Hazel awoke, she saw Isambard standing at the foot of her bed.

He wore the same black suit, white shirt, shiny brown shoes, and black bow tie that he wore last night, and he was waving a little flag that said 'Good morning' in neat, red letters.

'Good morning,' he said, by way of explanation. 'Did you sleep well?'

Hazel rubbed her eyes and sat up. She thought it was a bit rude waking her up like this. Her mouldy red curtains were still drawn, and she had no idea of the time.

'Yeah . . . fine. Hello.'

'Hello. I'm sorry we didn't chat much last night. I was . . .'

'Revising?'

'Yes . . . I was revising. Just like a normal boy. I hope the bed was OK?'

'I slept fine. Could I have some breakfast?'

'Sorry – Mrs Dungeon is very old, and doesn't get up until lunchtime. And Mother won't be up until noon.'

Isambard smiled slightly at this for some reason.

'But can't we just go and make ourselves breakfast? There must be some cereal or something.'

He laughed, as if he had never heard such a silly idea.

'Goodness! I don't think that would work. Your name is Hazel?'

'Yeah. We had dinner together last night. Remember?'

'Oh! I am sorry – I'm going about this all wrong.'

Isambard stood up very formally, and bowed.

'My name is Sir Isambard Pequierde, the Seventeenth Baronet Pequierde. I am, I believe, what is called your cousin. It means that your mother and my mother were sisters.' He smiled.

'Um . . . yes. I know what a cousin is. And, like I said, I've met you before.'

He looked apologetic.

'Oh! Sorry . . . um . . . I've really been looking forward to having someone my own age around the place . . . it can get a bit lonely here, and . . . well, I hope you have a nice time.'

He smiled sheepishly. Hazel had to admit it was nice to hear someone glad for her to be here. She only wished he'd said so last night.

'I thought we could do something fun on your first day . . . would you like to see my pets?'

Hazel loved pets, and if it turned out Isambard had a nice dog for her to play with, she might just be able to get through the next three weeks.

'That would be great! I'll just get dressed. Where shall I meet you?'

Isambard looked baffled for a moment.

'Oh! I see. You'd rather I left the room while you changed. Well, good luck putting your clothes on! I'll see you at the front door.'

With that, he put the flag down neatly onto the bed, turned quickly around, and sprinted clumsily out of the room, as fast as his little legs could carry him. Then, just a moment later, Hazel heard a loud crash as he fell down the stairs and landed on a tray.

'Don't worry, cousin! I'm all right. I just tripped as I was walking. My bones seem . . . yes, my bones are OK! I'll wait here!'

Hazel yawned. He was even weirder than Eugenia. Mind you – maybe he wasn't as boring, which would be something at least.

The weather was still grim outside. Though it was no longer raining, the sky was grey, and the grass was damp. The grounds of Eugenia's house were truly vast. It would take a good ten minutes to walk out to the barn, or the lake, or the forest, and her estate stretched out far beyond that.

Isambard was walking with a slight limp from his fall.

'I'm glad to have some company on my morning. I have quite a few pets to feed.'

'OK. What are we going to feed first?'

'I always feed the dog first.'

Brilliant! There was a dog! Maybe she was saved!

'His kennel's round the back of the house.'

There were some crumbling outhouses tucked away behind the kitchen, on the side of the house facing the barn, with six locked wooden doors, and a large kennel at the end of the row, painted with chipped black paint.

'What's his name?'

Isambard whistled and clapped his hands together.

'His name is Bullivant. He's a very special dog.'

Out of the kennel, Bullivant emerged, sleepy, wet, and not quite what Hazel had expected. Actually, she felt frightened.

'Isambard . . . is he supposed to look like that?'

Isambard looked a little hurt.

'Oh, my cousin, what do you mean? You don't think there's anything wrong with him? Haven't you seen a dog with a wooden head before?'

The eerie thing about Bullivant was that, having a wooden head, he didn't bark. Dogs normally make lots of noise, and love to say hello. But Bullivant said nothing. Other than the head, he was a normal, healthy black Labrador, with a nice red collar, a shiny coat, and a happy wagging tail. But where his floppy ears and runny nose should have been, was a bit of wood. It didn't look *unlike* a dog's head, but it certainly didn't look quite right either. The ears went straight up, and the mouth was just a line drawn on his snout. He had red circles painted on his cheeks, and the eyes had been drawn like a cartoon dog's, far too big, with long, girly eyelashes. You could also see the nails on his neck where the head had been hammered onto the body.

'Bullivant! Here, boy! Dinner!'

Bullivant wagged his tail, and bounded enthusiastically into the door of the shed.

Thump!

'Oh dear. Silly dog.' Isambard chuckled, picked him up off the ground, and patted his belly.

Hazel was almost as pale as Isambard now.

'How . . . how do you feed him?'

'Simple.'

Isambard reached under Bullivant, and pulled out a little tube, which Hazel guessed was connected to his stomach. He then produced a tube of tomato purée from his pocket, and began to squeeze it in. Bullivant wagged his tail.

'You feed him . . . tomato purée?'

'Oh, not always. He also enjoys garlic purée. And that cheese that comes in tubes — can't eat it myself, but he seems to like it.'

After feeding, Bullivant turned around, and walked into the wall of his kennel. If he was hurt, he had no whimpering noise with which to show it. Isambard picked him up again and put him in the kennel.

'Right. On to the ducks now.'

They began to walk towards the lake.

'Isambard, how did Bullivant get to be like that?'

Isambard looked proud.

'Oh, I did it myself. I didn't get any help from anyone.'

Hazel was appalled.

'What! How could you? How could you do something so cruel to that poor dog!'

Isambard looked hurt again.

'It was the only thing I could do after he had his head bitten off.'

Hazel stopped.

'Bitten off?'

But Isambard didn't seem to be paying attention, and he skipped down the hill toward the lake. Hazel hurried to catch up with him, though she wasn't at all happy about the whole dog business.

* * *

The lake was dark green and full of weeds. It was huge. Hazel wasn't even sure she'd be able to swim across it, so far away was the distant shore. As she looked to that shore, Hazel could make out some birds.

She tried to see the bright side of Isambard giving his dog a wooden head.

'Well . . . I suppose you gave him that wooden head to be nice. I'm amazed he's still alive, though.'

Isambard began to quack.

There was the sound of wings on the other side, and the birds started to fly clumsily toward them, only leaving the water for a few seconds at a time. Isambard produced some bread from his pocket.

'I love feeding the ducks.'

The ducks weren't really what she was expecting either.

For a start, ducks aren't supposed to smoke. Not just because it's very bad for them, and not just because they don't have any money to buy cigarettes, but because they *can't* smoke – they're ducks.

But, as it turned out, the ducks were breathing nicotine

merrily through the little holes on the tops of their yellow beaks. And even if they didn't have any money, they somehow had plenty of cigarettes. They were pretty white ducks, and they numbered thirty or forty, a third of which were little ducklings.

' . . . Um . . . Isambard, I really don't think it's good for ducks to be smoking.'

Isambard seemed genuinely surprised at this.

'But what else can I do? These ducks are very stressed. I gave them the cigarettes to calm them down.'

'What! That's terrible! My mum said that when she smoked cigarettes they never really calmed her down at all — the only stress they relieve is the stress of not having a cigarette!'

Isambard had stopped throwing bread to the ducks. He looked upset.

'I'm doing the best I can. I'm not a psychiatrist. I don't know how to deal with the extreme mental trauma these ducks have been through!'

'What extreme mental trauma? They're ducks!'

At this Isambard looked a little calmer. He had clearly decided that Hazel was just too stupid to understand.

'You'd be traumatised too if you had been to war. These ducks are the last surviving members of their fleet. All the others were killed. They have seen hundreds of comrades die. They are missing eyes, and legs, and wings. These precious cigarettes are the only thing that keeps them going.'

With that, he started to walk away.

'Where are you going?'

'To feed the pigs. You can come if you like.'

Once again, Isambard calmed down very quickly. He seemed to be used to people criticising him. By the time they arrived at the other side of the house on the side facing the forest, it was as if they had never argued at all. On the way to the forest was a small, fenced-in enclosure. It had a wooden hut at one end, and there was hay strewn over the ground.

Isambard produced a carrot from his pocket.

'Jilly! Jerry! Breakfast!'

A dark grey pig, half the size of Bullivant, poked its head out of the hut.

'Oink!'

Then another, identical pig stuck its head out.

'Oink!'

Seeing the carrot, they both dashed out to eat. However, their movements were very clumsy. Whereas two normal, healthy pigs would have eight legs between them, Jilly and Jerry had only seven. But it was not Jilly that was missing a leg, or Jerry that was missing a leg. They shared a leg – Jilly's back left one, or Jerry's front right one, depending on how you looked at it. They scrambled with difficulty to the carrot, and grabbed an end each and bit it in half.

'Oh my!' exclaimed Hazel, 'I've never seen Siamese twins before.'

Isambard seemed confused.

'Siamese twins?'

' . . . Um . . . yeah, Siamese twins. They were born sharing a leg, right?'

'Oh, no — I did that.' Isambard smiled. 'I'm afraid Jerry lost his leg just like Bullivant lost his head — so the only way to deal with it was to have him share one with his sister. Or was it Jilly who lost the leg?'

For the third time this morning, Hazel was appalled.

'What! Why didn't you just give Jerry a wooden leg — or Jilly — or whoever? The way you've done it, neither of them can walk!'

'Now, now, cousin, don't hurt their feelings — the twins can walk pretty well given that they lost a leg.'

Hazel was beginning to lose her temper.

'They didn't lose a leg! One of them lost a leg, and then you stuck them together! I think you've been very cruel to these pets!'

Isambard looked at her with his big, brown eyes. He apparently hadn't been expecting this. He started crying. Hazel, who had been about to shout at him some more, suddenly felt very bad. She patted him on the back.

'. . . Sorry . . . I think you need to calm down.'

'Don't you tell me to calm down! You know what? Bite me!'

This was not the sort of thing she expected Isambard to say. It wasn't a very posh thing to say at all.

'I beg your pardon?'

'Bite me,' said Isambard through the tears.

Hazel held her head in her hands, exhausted and annoyed.

'What does that mean, Isambard? That's just something you heard an American say on TV . . .' although it was hard to imagine Isambard watching TV.

'I know. They have a TV at my school, and I watch it sometimes and the people I see on it are all very cool, and when cool people want to tell someone stupid to go away, they say "Bite Me", and now I say it too.'

Hazel shook her hands and jumped up and down.

'But you don't even know what it *means!*'

'I know exactly what it means! I'm daring you to bite me. But you're too frightened. You wouldn't dare bite my terrifying neck! Bite me if you dare! That's what it means. OOOOWW!!!!! GET OFF! GET OFF MY NECK!!'

Hazel let go of Isambard's neck, wiped her mouth, and sat grumpily down on the ground. She was sometimes surprised how quickly she lost her temper.

'I'm sorry, Isambard,' she fumed. 'I shouldn't have bitten your neck.'

'Ow . . . ow . . . oh, it hurts . . . it hurts!'

Isambard was holding his neck and rolling around on the ground. Hazel thought he was making a bit too much of a fuss.

'But you *were* daring me to bite it.'

After a moment, Isambard stopped rolling about, and sighed with deep resignation. He rubbed his neck, and clambered back up to standing as if nothing had happened.

It was amazing – Hazel could well have expected to be in all sorts of trouble for biting him – but after his little outburst, he seemed to forget it instantly. She had completely lost it with him, and he'd calmed down in a matter of seconds.

Thinking about it later, Hazel decided it must be because of his mother. It made her sad to think of this pale, bookish boy living out in the middle of nowhere with his mother – with no father, or brothers, or sisters to protect him. She would have abused him, berated him, and belittled him every day of his life – from the moment he woke up to the moment he went to bed. Over time he must have got used to it. Years of insults and abuse had taken their toll, and even Hazel's most extreme fits of temper would be nothing compared to what he was used to. It didn't look like Hazel was going to be able to do anything mean enough to upset the son of a woman like Eugenia.

'Yes, Hazel, I'm sorry too – we shouldn't be arguing when we're supposed to be having a holiday.'

Hazel looked back to the house.

'I think I'd like to go back now.'

Isambard nodded enthusiastically.

'Yes! Going inside's a good idea. We'll go back to the house and get some lunch. Then I can do my revision, and you can do whatever it is you came here to do.'

Hazel thought to herself that she hadn't come here to *do* anything. She had been *made* to come here.

* * *

'Well, children,' said Eugenia with a grimace. 'What have you been up to today?'

Isambard smiled timidly.

'I fed my animals, with my cousin's help, and then did my revision until lunch was called.'

This brought Eugenia not even the tiniest flicker of joy or interest.

'I see. You like animals, do you, Walnut?'

Hazel breathed in, and counted to ten.

'It's Hazel, actually, and yes I do like animals. However. I really don't think that the ducks should be allowed to smoke.'

Eugenia appeared bored.

'Ducks? What ducks? What are you raving about, child?'

'The ducks in the lake. They've been smoking . . . the ducks . . . smoking . . . um . . .'

Eugenia seemed to have lost interest. Hazel tried to eat some of her 'mashed potato', but it was so lumpy that really it should have just been called 'potato'. When she had told Aunt Eugenia she was a vegetarian she must not have been listening, because she got chicken for lunch. In lumpy gravy. Isambard, when Mrs Dungeon handed him his food, tucked in heartily.

The dining room was opposite the drawing room, and would have been a grand, sumptuous room, were it not for the pigeons nesting in the ceiling. The north wall was completely covered in their white, sticky poop. The dining table was long and wonky, with bits missing in the middle. The chairs were mismatched. The plates were old and chipped.

'The very idea of an animal smoking is preposterous. I mean – how could they possibly hold a cigarette in their beaks!'

This was very strange. Could Eugenia care so little about her own estate that she didn't know the ducks were smokers? Or was she trying to make Hazel cross?

Hazel looked to Isambard, expecting him to inform his mother that he had, in fact, for some mysterious reason, got all the ducks hooked on cigarettes. But he said nothing. Just like last night he sat there, silent, unless Eugenia addressed him directly. He had been very different that morning – odd, maybe, but at least talkative. Didn't he tell his mother anything?

'You agree, don't you, Isambard? The very idea of a smoking duck is nonsense.'

At this question, Isambard finally responded. He put down his forkful of 'mashed' potato, and turned with frightened eyes to his mother.

'Human beings are the only species that smokes cigarettes,' he said.

Hazel gawped in shock.

'See! Isn't Isambard clever! The only species! See, Peanut? You've been caught telling just the sort of fib that stupid people tell – a fib that makes no sense!'

Eugenia's lip curled in an expression that looked almost like pleasure, but not quite. Victorious, her attention wandered away again.

Hazel couldn't believe it! Only a few hours ago, Isambard had been insisting that cigarettes were essential to the ducks' happiness, but in front of his mother he'd denied it was even possible. She tried to catch his eye, in the hope of understanding why he was lying.

After a moment, he saw her. As he looked at her, he seemed sad – almost as if he wanted to say sorry for making Hazel look silly in front of his mother. He sighed a little sigh, and looked away again.

When they had finished eating, he drifted off to his room, and Hazel didn't see him again until dinner.

* * *

In the afternoon, Hazel was alone. Isambard was revising at the top of the house and Eugenia sat in the drawing room. Mrs Dungeon busied herself with dinner, while Mr Pude helped Boynce move fresh logs into the barn. Bullivant was in his kennel, the ducks on their lake, and Jilly and Jerry in their pen.

Hazel, utterly lost as to what to do with herself, sat on the edge of her bed, swinging her legs. She even ended up brushing her teeth she was so bored. It was too grey to go for another walk. She was not sleepy, and did not feel like a nap. There was — and I cannot stress this enough — no television.

She stood up, went over to the window, and stared out of it.

Yup.

That tree was still there.

And all the grass.

And those bushes.

In fact, the view from her window had not changed, even slightly, in the four full minutes since she last checked it. Probably time to go back to the bed and sit down again.

The problem with boredom is that it is infectious. If one is in an excited mood, anything one experiences seems exciting too. If the sun is shining and the world is on your side, jumping up and down on the spot can seem like an adventure. Somebody saying hello can bring a tear of joy to your eye. Tidying your room can seem like a quest fit for a hero. But when you are bored, all the world becomes boring too. Jumping up and down on the spot becomes tiring and pointless. The person who said hello secretly hates you. Tidying your room is a task so insurmountably impossible that the house will fall down before you manage it. So, given her present mood, if the Emperor of Japan had teleported into her room and asked her she'd like to go on a dragon ride to the moon, she'd probably have told him she couldn't be bothered.

If only to keep herself awake, Hazel stood up and walked out of her room.

So.

Here she was.

Outside of her room.

Brilliant.

Her room was on the first floor of the west wing of the house, and her door was the third on the right. The *third*. Of *three*. Just on one *side*. That made six rooms on the first floor of the west wing. And the same again on the east wing. Which, if there were the same number of rooms on every floor (which there weren't, but Hazel was not a natural geographer) meant there were forty-eight rooms in the house. Not to mention the towers and the cellar.

None of these rooms contained anything at all to do.

But, given that Hazel was familiar with her bedroom, and the corridor outside her bedroom by now, maybe checking some of the other rooms couldn't hurt. She set off aimlessly, and surveyed her surroundings. As she ambled down the corridor, the cobwebs seemed like old news. The wine stains on the walls were exactly what she expected. It was obvious that there would be a sparrow living in the grandfather clock.

The paintings on the walls showed generation after

generation of square-jawed men with thick black hair. Some were in armour, ready for war. Others stood elegantly with poodles in front of the house. Others were proudly showing off scientific equipment. All of them needed a good clean.

Hazel decided that she might as well go to the third door on the right of the east wing of the house. Not because it would be particularly fun, but because there was no real point in going anywhere, and she might as well visit that room as any other. She passed the great oak staircase, and the giant mirror in the middle of the corridor that hadn't shown anyone what their face looked like in years. Unless your face was large, flat, and covered in dust – which seems unlikely.

The east wing was much the same. Unpolished, dark, wooden floors. Peeling wallpaper. A grandfather clock with a sparrow in it – no, wait – this one had a crow. Exactly opposite where her door stood was an identical door. Hazel, though she could not imagine anything interesting being behind it, opened the door.

The room was much like her own, but with no bed or wardrobe. Instead there was a long table, a desk under the window, and bookshelves along the walls.

'Great', thought Hazel. 'I feel riveted.'

It was, she supposed, a study. The shelves stopped at intervals, leaving room for a few small photographs. The desk was wide and sturdy, with a green felt top. The long table was covered in books. She inspected one of them. It was bound in black leather, and entitled 'Tanzania'. It sat on top of an identical book entitled 'Kenya'. It hadn't been read in years.

Laid out on the desk was a thick address book, containing a list of people living in Tanzania. Some had English-looking names, others African-looking ones. The addresses had been written by someone with handwriting even worse than Hazel's. Names were written incorrectly, crossed out, then rewritten. Ink-splotches peppered the page. There were foreign coins scattered near the book, and a brass statue of what Hazel thought must be a wildebeest stood proudly at the corner of the desk.

It was only when she looked at the photographs that Hazel understood. This was the first time she had seen the face of Sir Podbury Pequierde.

He was a handsome man. His skin was tanned and glowing — with dimples in his cheeks and chin. His curly black hair was thick and shiny, if a little grey at the temples. His straight, noble nose sat between two flashing eyes. His moustache was as strong and commanding as the wildebeest on the desk.

Every photograph was of him, and every photograph had been taken in Africa. The room must have been a special study for his safari trips. Hazel knew Podbury had loved East Africa — or, had loved the part of East Africa with massive, exciting animals in it. He must have planned his trips from here, and the address book must contain the details of people he knew out in Tanzania . . . Tanzania . . . where Mount Kilimanjaro was! That was where he had married Eugenia. Poor man.

The photographs on the walls were very blurry. You could just about make out what was going on in each one — Podbury was always in the foreground, grinning madly, and in the background was some exciting creature. In the first was a wildebeest like the one on the desk, armed with terrifying horns, and as tall as Podbury. He could only have been a few feet away from it, and was giving a thumbs-up to the camera. He also seemed to be holding a glass of wine.

There were other photos with other animals – a crocodile, a hippo, a zebra – and in each photo his pose was the same. He stood very close to the animal, smiling from ear to ear, with a thumb in the air. Although sometimes he was holding a gin and tonic rather than wine.

Hazel imagined that if she'd been there, she'd have been pleading with him to not go so close to the beasts. She imagined the crocodile snapping its jaws, or the zebra kicking its legs, while she begged Podbury to move further away – or at least put down his drink. Those trips must have been a nightmare – Podbury always drunk, always in danger.

It must have been this love of danger that brought him so close to the tiger enclosure at London Zoo – close enough to fall in and end his safari trips for ever.

With the death of this dashing man, the Pequierde fortune had died too. The crow in the clock outside was proof, if proof be needed, that none of the family's fabulous riches remained. He had spent it all on gambling, and drinking, and expensive trips to Tanzania.

But not on a bloody television. He'd bought plenty of entertainment for himself, but what was *Hazel* supposed to do for the next three weeks? Stare at maps of Kenya?

Hazel turned away from the photographs in disgust,

stormed out of the room, and slammed the door. Then she went back to her room, sat on her bed, and stared into space for a full hour, whilst daydreaming of being somewhere else.

Eventually supper happened, and Hazel endured another hour of abuse from Eugenia, silence from Isambard, and gravy so thick you could plaster ceilings with it. After that ordeal, she went back to her room for another exciting bout of wall-staring, and at nine o'clock, with nothing better to do, she put herself to bed.

She was only one day into her holiday.

The Fourth Chapter of this Book

So that was how it seemed Hazel would spend her holiday – in abject boredom, killing the hours between meals as best she could. Days dripped by. She went out with Isambard to his pets every morning – but by the end of lunch he had usually gone up to his room. Eugenia was hardly seen between meals, and Hazel had no intention of looking for her. The dust, and the mushrooms, and the square-jawed men staring down from the walls became normal to Hazel. The long, dark corridors were her whole world. Her real home was a distant memory.

The weather made no improvement. Vast, grey skies rolled over the house, occasionally heaving torrents of rain upon it, occasionally darkening with thunder, but never once opening to reveal the sun. Deprived of sun, the grounds of the Pequierde estate cooled. As each day became a little chillier, Hazel felt less inclined to leave the house, and with each day of rain the house became more damp, and the gross odour of mould and mildew was everywhere. Boynce made repairs to the leaking roof and the flooded cellar, but the house was, fundamentally, sick. Bullivant never came out from his kennel, the ducks sat shivering beneath a tree, and Jilly and Jerry were prisoners in their hut. Hazel found herself sitting for hours in front of her window in that smelly, decrepit, boring house, staring out at the rain, without hope of anything better to do.

This was her summer holiday.

If she'd had a friend here, maybe it would have been better. But she didn't have any friends, so that put a stop to that idea. Isambard was around, but although he was always polite, he was a strange boy, and Hazel barely knew what to say to him. He did, at least, make the effort to suggest new things — but they weren't very good suggestions. They were things like flying a kite during a thunderstorm, or diving to the bottom of the lake to collect samples of sea-weed and mud, or trying to figure out how large the Pequierde estate was by walking around it counting their footsteps, and then checking how accurate their estimate was on a map. Now, maybe some children get excited about words like 'thunderstorm', 'seaweed', and 'estimate', but Hazel was not one of them. She said 'no' as politely as she could, and instead went up to her room to do absolutely nothing at all.

Finally, however, on a morning like all the others, Isambard came up with a decent idea.

'Hazel, after we've fed Jilly and Jerry, perhaps you'd like to visit the games room?'

Games room! Why had Hazel not been told about the

games room! She accepted instantly, and Isambard agreed to take a break from revising that afternoon.

Lunch with Eugenia was, as always, excruciating. Today she accused Hazel of being a 'pimple-nosed simpleton', and told her that the world would be a better place if all the stupid people were rounded up and put on an island somewhere to leave all the intelligent people alone. Hazel found herself imagining being flown away to that peaceful, sun-kissed island of morons, and lying back on the beach, while all around her friendly, dim people fell over things, set fire to themselves, and tried to eat sand. Heaven.

Then, when Eugenia finished, she went upstairs to get a book for an afternoon of sitting in her armchair. Isambard winked to Hazel, and said 'Follow me, cousin — into the drawing room before she comes downstairs!'

The drawing room was just as grimy and frightening as it had been on Hazel's first night. They scurried over to the far corner, under the stuffed head of a badger, and Isambard pushed at a stretch of wall (which looked like any other stretch of wall) to reveal a hidden door. They hopped through, and he closed the door as quietly as possible.

They were in a place as big as the drawing room, on the opposite side of the house. All the curtains were drawn, and Hazel could barely see a thing. Isambard seemed very happy to be showing her this hidden place. He ran over to the large set of curtains that faced out towards Jilly and Jerry's pen, and opened them.

White light fell on the dark forms in the room — and made visible a pool table, a roulette wheel, a bar well stocked with wine and spirits, a dart board, and a card table. It was all very grand. The pool table must have been the death of several enormous trees, and the life's work of several carpenters — it had what seemed like a forest of carved animals under it, inlaid with ivory and gold. The roulette wheel was similarly carved, with antelope horns sticking inconveniently out of its legs. The dartboard was set into a beautiful expanse of mahogany panelling. The bar, on closer inspection, was not so well stocked — for although it had a wall of bottles behind it, each one was empty.

Podbury must have lost thousands of pounds in this room.

'This is amazing. Do you and your mum never come here?' said Hazel.

Isambard perched on one of the chairs at the card table.

'No, Mother hasn't used it for years. I don't think the servants bother to clean it,' he said.

They certainly didn't bother to clean it. Not only was everything covered in a thick layer of cobwebs, but all the games seemed to have been left in the middle of being used. There were four hands of cards at the table, and piles of chips at the roulette wheel, and darts in the dartboard, and balls on the pool table. All of these things had been here long enough for several generations of spiders to decide that it would be a sensible place to make a home, settle down and start a family. In fact, was that a mouse poking its head out of the dartboard?

'Wow! This is great. Do you want to play cards or darts first? I don't know how to play roulette or pool,' said Hazel.

Isambard looked confused.

'Oh. Well, I don't know how to play roulette or pool either – or cards or darts for that matter . . .'

He clearly hadn't expected Hazel to want to *play* the games.

'What do you mean? Haven't you ever played with any of this stuff?'

'No – never.'

'What? Not even with your dad . . . um . . . I mean . . . sorry . . .'

Hazel suddenly felt very embarrassed.

'No, no, it's OK, Hazel. I never played any of these games with him. And Mother doesn't do anything like play games these days.'

'Right. Sorry. Well, would you like to play cards? It could be fun – since you've taken the afternoon off revising?'

'Yes – yes, that would be nice. But, as I said, I don't know any rules, and I don't think Mother would either.'

Hazel had a look at the card table. How hard could it be? She'd spent hours happily playing snap with her mum, and once they'd even played gin rummy. Yes – gin rummy – that would be good! She wiped the cobwebs off the cards and gathered the pack together. Now she just needed to remember how to play.

'Right, now listen up, Isambard – I'll explain how to play gin rummy, which is a really good game. OK?'

'OK.'

'Good. Now, we start with five . . . no, seven . . . no . . . um . . . we start with half the pack each,' she gave Isambard half the pack without shuffling it, 'and the winner is the person with the most . . . no, the least . . . no . . . all the red cards at the end of the game,' she flashed a diamond at him so that he understood, 'and to win them we put a card each in the middle of the table and whichever is the highest . . . no, the lowest . . . no . . . whichever is an even number wins.'

They both put down a card. Isambard put down the nine of clubs, Hazel put down the five of hearts.

'Right . . . so, if neither of us puts down an even number, then whoever has the highest card puts down another card.'

Isambard put down the three of spades.

'Right . . . and because you have two cards, and I only have one, you . . . um . . . win.'

Isambard smiled and collected all the cards.

'No! Wait . . . I think the person who loses gets the cards.'

Isambard cheerfully handed them over to her.

' . . . And . . . because I've got more cards, I get to put down two cards this time.'

She put down the seven of hearts and the nine of hearts. Isambard put down the queen of spades.

'Right. And because I have more cards, I win . . . so you get all the cards.'

'But . . . is the queen an even or odd number?'

Hazel thought for a second.

'Well, she's not a number at all, and besides I have more cards.'

'Oh, OK — so now we have the same number of cards again — but because I lost I put down two cards, which . . .

50

um . . . means I win . . . whatever cards we put down . . . so you pick up the cards . . . which means you put down two on the next go . . . which means you win . . .'

Isambard paused.

'Um . . . doesn't this mean that neither of us will ever win and the game will never end?'

Hazel threw her cards at the dartboard, which drew a squeak of complaint from the mouse.

'Yes, ALL RIGHT, so I got the rules wrong!'

There was an awkward pause, before Isambard tried to smooth things over.

'Maybe we should play darts?'

'NO! I want to play cards – you must have a book of card game rules!'

'Well, no, we don't actually – I think Dad was worried that if his friends could look up the rules they might get better at it than him – not that he ever won anyway.'

Hazel groaned.

Well, if there was one person who would know the rules it would be Hazel's mum. Hazel hadn't spoken to her for days, which felt strange. Maybe she could phone her? She definitely had the number of her hotel in Egypt!

'Hey! Could I use your phone to call my mum – she'd know the rules!'

Isambard looked slightly shocked.

'Well, there's a phone in the drawing room, but you'll have to ask my mum if you can use it.'

'Great! We'll go and ask her now.' With this Hazel made for the door into the drawing room.

'Stop! Mum wouldn't want us to be in this room! I was

going to say we should wait until dinner time and sneak out then . . .'

'What!? We're supposed to wait in here playing a card game that neither of us can win and that never ends until dinner!'

'Well . . . we could play darts?'

Hazel groaned, and threw herself on the floor.

'I don't *want* to play darts, I want to play *cards!*'

She sighed, and lay there on the mouldy carpet for a moment. She thought that she would rather just sit and stare out of the window than play darts with a boy who didn't even know the rules. She got up, went over to the window, and sat down, with the intention of not talking to Isambard until dinner. After a painful silence, it occurred to her that Isambard had only been trying to be nice, and that she should try to look on the bright side.

'Well, I suppose I can just ask your mother if I can use the phone over dinner, and we can play cards tomorrow.'

Isambard looked worried.

'Oh, I don't think that would be a very good idea . . . it's . . . it's best not to ask Mum for anything at dinner. I don't know if you've noticed, but she can be a little grumpy in the evening. Probably best to ask at lunch tomorrow.'

Hazel screamed, ran over to the dartboard, picked up a dart, and threw it at Isambard's head. Luckily he ducked, and it landed in the leg of the pool table.

'I HATE THIS HOUSE! I HATE IT! What do you mean your mum's "a little grumpy in the evening"! She's always grumpy! I just want to call *my* mum!'

Isambard was cowering behind the pool table now, too

frightened to speak. Hazel took a few deep breaths, and
went over to sit by the window again.

'Sorry,' mumbled Isambard from under the pool table,
eventually.

They sat in that room, saying nothing to each other for
hours.

* * *

Hazel decided to take Isambard's advice and not ask
Eugenia over dinner, so another evening, and night, and
morning passed without anything exciting happening at all.
Which meant that by lunch the next day Hazel was so desperate to speak to her mum she thought she might burst.
All she needed was *one* thing, one little bit of fun, and then
she might stop herself from losing her mind this summer.

It was very hard to wait as lunch was served up. Heaps
of soggy sprouts were poured onto her plate, Eugenia
curled up in her chair looking miserable, and the pigeons
cooed menacingly in the ceiling. The food was as disgusting as ever, and Isambard was, as ever, silent.

Eugenia's white hair seemed matted today. Usually it
flared up out of the side of her head like a firework, but
now it was flat and tangled against her scalp. She must have
fallen asleep in her armchair that morning. Her terrible
eyes were dull today, yes, but no less fearful. Hazel never
looked into those eyes, because she thought a jet of flame
might leap out of them at any moment.

'Aunt Eugenia . . .'

Those flaming eyes shot round towards her, and she
looked down at her sprouts.

'That's Lady Pequierde to you.'

What on earth was she talking about? Hazel had always called her Aunt Eugenia. If her niece wasn't allowed to call her Aunt Eugenia, who was?

'You could do with learning some manners. If one has no brains, no friends, and no charm, one must at least have manners.'

Hazel thought back to when she had lost her temper with Isambard in the games room. Although she probably shouldn't have thrown a dart at his head, she felt certain that calling someone brainless, friendless, and charmless was much worse. Even if it was true.

'Sorry, Lady Eugenia . . .'

'Oh, for heaven's sake! Why must you crawl to me like that? Aunt Eugenia will do perfectly well, you don't need to go calling me "your highness" or anything — it certainly won't make me like you.'

Hazel clenched her fists in rage.

'But you *just* said . . .'

' . . . I am perfectly aware of what I have and have not said, Wingnut. Now, if you don't have anything intelligent to say, stop talking.'

Hazel thought she was about to put her thumb through her hand she was clenching her fists so tight. Who did Eugenia think she was? She hadn't even been born a Lady, she'd just married one. Or a Lord — she'd married a Lord — that's what Hazel meant. You could never call a man a lady when he had a moustache like Podbury's.

'But, please, I just wanted to ask one thing . . .'

' . . . You have *already* asked a great deal of me by asking me to listen to you whilst I am eating my lunch. If you ask me for something, it will be the second thing you have asked for.'

Hazel counted to ten and tried to stay calm.

'Well, sorry, the second thing I wanted to ask for, was whether, if it's at all possible, I could, maybe, please, use the telephone to call my mum.'

Some shadow passed across Eugenia's face. Her eyes, still hateful, were for a time also sad. She turned away and looked out at the pouring rain.

'Certainly not. What an absurd request. Never bother me with something like this over lunch again.'

Hazel was ready to cry.

'But . . .'

'But me no buts, young lady. What could you possibly need to call your mother for?'

'For, for, for . . .'

' . . . Stammering is a sign of mental stupidity, and besides don't answer back.'

'But you asked me a question!'

At this, Eugenia suddenly stood up. Hazel felt that the sprouts might catch fire any moment, so intense was Eugenia's rage.

'NEVER raise your voice at my table.'

That was all she said. She stared at Hazel for a moment, then sat down.

Hazel said nothing else for the whole meal. Isambard neither spoke nor looked in her direction, and when he had finished eating, he ran upstairs to his room before she could speak to him. Eugenia wandered away to the drawing room, and Hazel stormed outside to stand in the rain while she cried.

* * *

Behind the house, Hazel stamped her foot in a rage, and shrieked as loud as she could. She was soaking wet, and her trainers were covered in mud. She planned on screaming for at least the next two hours.

Suddenly she heard a thumping sound.

She spun round, to see Bullivant emerging from his kennel, his tail thwacking against the wood. Although Bullivant could not hear her, or see her, or smell her, he must have felt the vibrations in the ground as she was stamping her foot. Did he know that she was Hazel, and not Isambard? Did he know that she had not come to feed him?

He walked courageously out towards her, slipping in the mud as he went, but miraculously reached her, and rubbed his wooden head against her hand. His tail wagged happily, and, finding that she was not going to feed him, he sat patiently beside her.

Did he think she needed him? Did he need her for some reason?

She began to tickle behind his ear, but of course he could not feel it. She reached down to rub his shoulders, and scratch his neck. He was soaked through too, now, and Hazel began to worry about his head getting damp. What if it rotted?

This was a stupid house. Eugenia probably didn't even know her dog had no head, and if she had known she wouldn't have cared.

Hazel felt calmer now. She was breathing normally, and hadn't stamped her foot for two minutes. Her mind began to clear. Maybe she just needed to try again. Eugenia couldn't possibly stop her from speaking to her own mother — she just had to explain herself more clearly. If she patiently told Eugenia that she needed to find out the rules of gin rummy, she'd have to accept it.

Bullivant nuzzled her leg. She realised she was shivering, and it was time to go inside. She gave him a final pat on his head (which made a hollow thunking sound) and went back inside.

She had a couple of hours to think about what she was going to say, sitting up in her room, and after that she went down to dinner. She tried to look as sweet, calm, and well-behaved as possible, and tried to think happy thoughts, about sunshine, and picnics, and tennis.

Eugenia looked even worse. Her face was red from lying against a cushion, and her hair was a state. She did not give any sign that she remembered arguing with Hazel a few hours ago, but instead gazed off into nowhere.

Hazel cleared her throat, sat up straight, and began.

'Aunt Eugenia — Lady Pequierde — I was wondering if it would be possible for me to ask you a question.'

Eugenia looked over, and tried for a moment to find fault with what Hazel had said, but gave up.

' . . . Very well.'

Hazel smiled sweetly.

'I was wondering if there was any way I might be allowed to use the telephone . . .'

'No.'

'. . . because . . .'

'No.'

'. . . because I would like to ask my mother the rules of gin rummy.'

'Absolutely not.'

Eugenia looked blankly at Hazel.

'. . . Well, I'd really appreciate it because . . .'

'No.'

'. . . I'll be here for three weeks . . .'

'Oh God, don't remind me.'

'. . . and if I knew the rules to gin rummy I could play it with Isambard, because you see I've been quite bored . . .'

'You are bored because you are boring.'

'. . . and there's no telly, and the weather's terrible, and I'd really like something to do.'

'Besides, we don't have any cards.'

This stumped Hazel a bit.

'Yes, you do . . .'

'Where?'

'. . . Well, in the games room . . .'

And in a flash Eugenia was standing.

'How do you know that! How dare you!? You've been sneaking around my house! You've been spying on me . . .'

'. . . no . . .'

'. . . don't LIE! I have a spy in my house, and she's sneaking around in rooms she's not supposed to go in! Who said you could go into that room!'

'. . . no one . . .'

'EXACTLY. You will not be allowed to phone your mother as long as you are here. When your mother does arrive here, she will be told that you are a liar and sneak, and that she needs to take a firmer hand with you by far!'

'. . . please . . .'

'That is FINAL! My name is Eugenia, Lady Pequierde, and I will not be trifled with by a ten-year-old girl! You are under my roof, and you will obey me!'

With this, Eugenia picked up Hazel's plate, and flung it at the wall. Then she picked up her mug of tea, and flung that at the wall as well. Then she left the room. Isambard, unable to look at Hazel, let out a whimpering sound, and ran upstairs.

She sat alone in the room for a moment, stunned. Then there was a knocking outside the door, and Mrs Dungeon entered, looking concerned.

'Oh, dear, has her ladyship gone and lost her temper again?'

Hazel only ever saw Mrs Dungeon at meal times. She was a kindly old lady, just as round as Pude the butler, and even smaller. She wore a pink apron, an old white dress, and a pair of thick glasses that made her eyes look massive. Her hair was dyed an unconvincing shade of red. She definitely had the look of someone who only got up at lunchtime.

Pude emerged behind her, and put a friendly hand on her shoulder.

'Has she gone and dropped that mug again? Oh dear. Maybe I should bring her a biscuit.'

'Are you all right there, little girl? I hope you weren't scared by the mug.'

No, thought Hazel, there are plenty of things to be scared of besides the mug.

'Would you like a nice hot chocolate?'

Hazel groaned. Mrs Dungeon was always offering hot chocolate, but when she went to the kitchen to get it she could never find any. She was a nice old lady – but very forgetful.

'Well, I would, but I didn't think there was any.'

'Isn't there? What a pity. Maybe I can find you some gravy.'

This was something else Mrs Dungeon had a tendency to do. She had somehow got it into her head that the next best thing to hot chocolate was a mug of gravy.

'Go on dear, a nice mug of gravy'd do you good!'

'No! I'm . . . um . . . I'm fine without.'

'Oh go on, it's nearly as nice as hot chocolate!'

Hazel thought Mrs Dungeon's gravy was, if anything the exact opposite of hot chocolate. She certainly didn't think it would 'do her any good', given that it was as thick as cement and tasted of shoes. So, Mrs Dungeon was a nice old lady, but very forgetful, and with a very unrealistic idea of how much other people wanted to eat her gravy. That is to say, she thought other people wanted to eat her gravy. They did not.

'No, really – that's all right. I shouldn't have gravy because . . . um . . . it gives me nightmares.'

'Oh, me too, dear; gravy will give you vivid dreams if you have too much of it.'

Hazel felt very queasy at the idea of eating 'too much' gravy. She thought any gravy was too much. How much did Mrs Dungeon think was too much? A pint? Two pints? A bucket?

'I say, dear, you don't know what Lady Piquierde was angry about do you?'

Hazel was too furious to talk about it.

'No! I have no idea.'

'Oh, well, that's not unusual, dear. Sometimes she just flies off the handle and none of us knows why. But that's her ladyship! We'd best go and see if there's anything we can do to calm her down. I hope you're all right on your own. See you later!'

Hazel was most certainly *not* all right on her own. She wanted to speak to her mum! Not only had Eugenia forbidden her, but it didn't seem like anyone else in the house was going to be any help either.

She was alone again, and still stunned.

Hazel's mother never did anything like throwing plates at walls. It was not something Hazel was used to.

As she tried to work out what on earth to do, she noticed that her plate had hit a part of the wall that was already covered in pigeon poop, spraying sprouts and potatoes everywhere. The plate had, of course, been covered in gravy, and now that terrible gravy was mixing with the butter from the potatoes, and the poop on the wall, to create a sort of browny, whitey, buttery, poopy, gravyish mudslide.

Hazel began to cry again.

*　*　*

Hours later she was awake in bed, too angry to sleep, thinking what to do, when she heard a knock at her door. She was half afraid it would be Eugenia.

'Come in . . .'

It was Isambard, looking worried.

' . . . Hi . . .'

' . . . Hi . . .'

He shuffled about on his feet, and tugged at his sleeves. Hazel sat up, and turned on her bedside light.

' . . . Um . . . I just wanted to check you were all right.'

Hazel harrumphed.

'I'm fine thanks. You might like to know that I will not be offering your mother an apology of any kind.'

' . . . Oh. OK. I suppose that's . . . yeah . . .'

'More than that, I will be waking up early tomorrow morning, when she is still in bed, stealing the telephone out of the drawing room, sneaking it into an upstairs room with a phone line, and calling my mother. And if Eugenia doesn't like it she can lump it.'

Isambard nodded enthusiastically.

'Yeah, sure . . . good . . . maybe you should do that. Right.'

Unable to think of anything else to say, he straightened his bow tie, waved goodbye, and shuffled out the door.

Hazel smiled. She turned out the light, rolled over, and went to sleep happy. She was really looking forward to speaking to her mother tomorrow – but more than that, she was looking forward to disobeying Eugenia.

* * *

At eight in the morning, when no one in the Pequierde household was even close to being awake, Hazel jumped out of bed and tiptoed downstairs. It was a strange place in the mornings. Of course, the house was always very empty, and it wasn't as if there'd be football matches or dance contests going on when everyone woke up. But somehow, knowing that Eugenia was not sitting down-stairs in the drawing room made the whole building a lit-tle more peaceful.

As she stepped into the drawing room, Hazel was begin-ning to feel very proud of herself. The phone was right there in the corner of the room, dusty and black, and in a heart-beat she snatched it up and ran out to the staircase.

As quietly as possible she made her way to the room opposite her own, which she had noticed had a phone line. She plugged the wire into the wall, and took a piece of paper with her parents' number on it.

Ring, ring. Ring, ring.

Even though the ringing was happening right next to Hazel's ear, and no one else would be able to hear it, she still looked around cautiously.

Ring, ring. Ring . . .

' . . . Hello?'

'Mum!'

Hazel heard a sigh on the other end.

'Oh, darling, how lovely to hear from you! Me and your father were just about to go out.'

'I miss you, Mum.'

'Oh, sweetie, I miss you too. We've been here almost a week now, so we'll see you again in just over two weeks.'

This sounded like *far* too long.

'I know, Mum. I wanted you to tell me the rules of gin rummy.'

'Oh, yes, of course, how nice! Are you playing card games with Aunt Eugenia?'

'. . . um . . . sort of . . .'

'Well, I'm glad to hear it. Now, if I remember right . . .'

Hazel's mother managed to convey the rules fairly quickly, as Hazel wrote them down. They certainly made a lot more sense than what Hazel had come up with. It was such a relief to talk to someone sane again, and, what's more, now Hazel would have something to *do*. Phoning Mum had definitely been a good idea.

'Does that help, sweetie? I hope I made the rules clear enough.'

'Yes, Mum. Thanks.'

'Well, that's all right. Now, I'm afraid me and your father really need to get going to make sure we miss the crowds, so I'm going to have to say goodbye. But why don't you call again this evening? Then we can have a nice long chat.'

Hazel clenched her fist in frustration.

'But I *can't* call you tonight.'

Mum didn't know what to make of this.

'Why ever not, darling?'

'Because Aunt Eugenia won't let me! I'm not even supposed to be calling you now — I had to steal the phone!'

Hazel heard a deep sigh on the other end.

'Darling, it really upsets me that you are *still* making up stories about my sister . . .'

'. . . but . . .'

'But me no buts, young lady! I am so fed up with this! Can't you at least *try* to like her?'

Hazel was crying again. Why wouldn't Mum believe her?

'Mum, please, it's true . . .'

'Stop it! Honestly, Hazel, sometimes I think . . .'

But Hazel never got to find out what her Mum thought, because the line had gone dead. She was filled with a sudden sense of dread. As she put the phone down, she turned round to look behind her.

It was Eugenia.

She stood there in her dressing gown, holding the phone line she had pulled out of the wall. She was very tall when she stood up. Her white hair, first thing in the morning, rose so high up off her head that it brushed the ceiling. She was already wearing her black boots.

'Well. I think you'd better come with me.'

That was all she said, and she said it quietly. Her eyes burned like embers, and Hazel could not turn away from them. They shimmered with rage.

Hazel stood up, and walked out of the room. As she passed Eugenia, and brushed one of those black boots with her feet, she felt so scared she might be sick. Eugenia wouldn't kick her, would she?

'This way.'

Eugenia began to walk towards the staircase. Hazel followed, grateful to not have to look into those eyes. But where she expected Eugenia to walk down the stairs, she instead went up towards the second floor. Hazel could not bring herself to follow.

Eugenia turned.

'If you do not follow me up this staircase, you will be

in even more trouble than you are already in. And I can tell you, with complete certainty, that you are, right now, in more trouble than you have ever been in before in your life.'

Hazel gulped, and followed her. As they ascended the stairs, Eugenia's boots squeaked on the wooden steps.

Hazel realised her aunt was holding a key.

At the top of the stairs, they turned to the east wing, and walked to the end of the corridor. Eugenia put the key in a door, and as she opened it, from that door came a stench so foul Hazel thought she must be dreaming it.

'This was, once, my greenhouse. I am sad to say that I have rather neglected the plants in it since . . . since . . .'

She said no more, but pointed through the door. Hazel, though she thought she might be sick, knew, as she stared at those eyes that burned like suns, that she had to go in.

The glass ceiling was very high, and the far wall consisted of four great windows. Through them, Hazel could see down to where Bullivant's kennel stood. It was a strange place for a greenhouse – on the second floor, tucked away between two towers. Eugenia must have carried water, and plants, and soil up two flights of stairs.

It was like hell.

Years ago, the flowers had begun to rot. As they rotted, with no one to water them, insects gathered to eat them. With the insects, came bacteria, and mould, and mushrooms, and all the scavenging things that filled this house – but in quantities that defied belief. Plant pots contained thick surfaces of one kind of mould, with a pool of another kind of mould on top of that, and insect larvae living in that pool, and other insects feeding on those larvae.

The air was thick with the buzzing of a thousand flies. A few fortunate spiders ruled over great empires of cobwebs. On those cobwebs the flies died in numbers too overwhelming for the spiders to eat, and they were left to hang there like lanterns.

Where the old plants had sickened and died, weeds had sprung up – flown in on the wind through the smashed panes of glass. Handfuls of caterpillars fed on these tangled, ugly plants, until the caterpillars themselves were carried off to be eaten by ants.

A bird had died on the floor, and a horde of maggots were eating its eyes.

Hazel turned round to Eugenia, who was smiling.

'Oh, and by the way. In case you were wondering how I knew you were getting up early to steal my telephone – Isambard told me. I found him creeping away from your room last night, and it didn't take him more than a minute to admit everything. I thought it best to get up early myself and catch you in the act. Goodbye.'

With that she locked the door, and left.

Hazel was too frightened to cry. She grabbed an old trowel off the ground for protection, ran to a corner by the window, and hid her face in her hands.

That day the sun at last came out.

As its rays flooded in through the glass ceiling of the greenhouse, the heat began to rise. Soon, the rotting plants were releasing a festival of new smells, each one more awful than the last. Hazel held her nose, and crouched by the window, and shook with fury. She didn't dare open her mouth for fear of what might fly into it.

At about eleven o'clock, she saw Isambard come out to meet Bullivant — Isambard who had betrayed her. He stopped, briefly, and looked up to the greenhouse. She did not know if he could see her, but he must have known that she was there, and therefore he must have known what she was suffering. She had always known he was a coward, but now she knew he was a traitor too. She had no friends in this house, and no one to protect her. She couldn't even call her parents. She tried not to cry, because she was half afraid the flies would drink her tears.

At noon, when the sun was at its height, Hazel smelled a smell of death and decay so terrible she thought she would go mad.

From that point, she didn't know what was happening to her. She'd had nothing to eat or drink, and she could not go to the toilet. The heat was unbearable. As soon as she had swatted one fly from her body, another ten took its place. She knew only fear, and disgust, and time stretched on for ever.

* * *

As the sun went down, the door to the greenhouse opened, and Hazel crawled, shaking, into the corridor. She had been inside for almost twelve hours. Eugenia led her down to her bedroom, and shut the door.

Once Eugenia had gone, Hazel ran to the bathroom. She scrubbed desperately at her arms and face, until her skin was dry and red. She scoured her head with shampoo until her eyes stung. She brushed her teeth until her gums hurt. She scrubbed, and scoured, and brushed, and scrubbed, and scoured, and brushed, and scrubbed, and scoured, and brushed.

In the end she was too tired to wash any longer, but still she didn't feel clean. She didn't think she'd ever feel clean again. She ran back to her room, and lay down on the bed, exhausted. Her head was spinning with those terrible smells, and with anger, and fear, and loneliness. As she lay, shivering, on that bed, she knew one thing for certain.

She was going to run away.

The Fifth Chapter of this Book

Hazel had never run away before, and was not entirely certain how to go about it. Did she need a weapon? Should she steal a car? How much food should she bring?

As she sat alone at lunch the next day – Eugenia being still too angry to eat, and Isambard too embarrassed – she had a good old think about these issues. She concluded: Yes; Yes; and Lots. However, she also concluded: There Were No Weapons; She Didn't Know How to Drive; and She Didn't Have any Food. The best she could manage was scraping the last of her carrots into a handkerchief, and going up to her room to wait for nightfall.

It being summer, night took a few hours to come, giving Hazel plenty of time to sit and think about what Eugenia had done to her. Every time she imagined Eugenia's glowering eyes, she felt her heart beat faster, and her breathing become shallow. What had Mum done to deserve a sister like this?

After three hours of brooding, worrying and sniffling, night fell on that loathsome house. She threw on her coat, her rucksack, and the wellies she had brought with her. She knew there was a torch hanging from the coat rack in the front hall. Terrified, she tiptoed out of bed. Eugenia's room was on the floor above, and Hazel tried to move with perfect silence.

Without too much difficulty, she got to the hall, picked up the torch, and slipped out of the front door.

She hadn't been any further towards the woods than the pig pen, but she knew that they went on for miles behind the house. She could make out empty fields on the horizon beyond them, but she didn't know what secrets the woods themselves held.

She took a deep breath, and set off into the dense undergrowth.

The ground in the woods was muddy from the rain. The paths through the trees were hard to follow, and didn't seem to lead anywhere. The trees were lush and green from all the water, but Hazel didn't find it easy to appreciate them in the dark.

She pushed branches out of her way and tried to stay calm. If she could just get to the fields on the other side, she would find a road and some kind person would drive her away from here.

But the woods were very scary, and Hazel was only a little girl. As the trees began to scratch her cheeks, and as she had less and less idea of where she was, she felt a sinking feeling in her stomach that must have been the desire to turn back. She was only ten minutes away from the house, and she could still give up. No! — she shook her head, thought about the greenhouse, and kept going — straight into a puddle. Well, something in between a puddle and a pond.

Squelch! Her boots filled up with water and her socks soaked through in an instant. Hazel promised herself she wouldn't cry. She started to turn around, and immediately fell over into the mud.

She crawled out of the water, spitting muck from her mouth. Her hair was sticky and tangled from the dirty water, and one ear was full of sludge.

She reached up to support herself with a tree branch, and managed to put her whole arm into a patch of stinging nettles.

Now she was crying. She fished the torch out of the pond, and shone it over the woods to try and see some dock leaves — but it was too dark, and the plant life too thick. The nettle sting had begun to really hurt, and she put it back into the water to cool it down.

Then something bit her.

With that, Hazel screamed, and ran full pelt into the forest, having no idea where she was going. She knocked her knees into logs, and heard her coat tear on a thorn, but just kept running, straight into the darkness.

The only thing she could think of that would solve her predicament was if she just died, there in the woods, and let everyone else deal with getting her out of there once she was dead. Maybe that would make Eugenia say something nice about her. Come to think of it, probably not. Hazel dying would surely provoke a long tirade about the stupidity of the dead girl, and how Eugenia always knew she was no good.

With that in mind, Hazel resolved to just keep running, however much the nettle sting hurt.

That was before she saw the light.

It was faint at first — just a flicker on a couple of branches and a dim glow in the sky. The woods were very deep, and had kept the light hidden.

What could it be?

Seeing as the only other options Hazel currently faced were running into a dark thicket of trees or dying, she thought heading towards the light couldn't be so bad. She was even a little curious. Boynce the gardener, maybe?

She wiped the mud and twigs off her face, and set off towards the mysterious glow. The trees were very thick now, and it was hard to pick her way through the bushes. The light began to get brighter, and more distinctly orange. It reflected off the leaves of the trees, and danced across the ground. It was almost pretty. Hazel felt certain it was the light from a fire.

At the back of her mind was the possibility that someone dangerous might be at the fire, so she turned off her torch just in case. She wasn't *very* worried though. The person by the fire could hardly be much worse than Eugenia.

Then Hazel started to hear a voice. A strange, rumbling, deep voice, as if the trees were talking. Maybe there was an old man in the woods? The voice was rough, like Hazel's mother's sounded before she gave up smoking last year.

Hazel suddenly worried that she would find the ducks out in the woods, having started a forest fire with one of their cigarettes, and talking about what to do. She didn't think ducks would be much good at putting out a forest fire.

As she got closer and the voice got louder, Hazel decided it wasn't a forest fire. It clearly wasn't big enough, and surely the voice would be more worried. Then she heard some words distinctly.

'Sounds like . . . feet? Sounds like — Hoofs! No? Sounds like . . . ground? No, no, OK . . .'

That didn't sound like the ducks. It was a very gravelly voice indeed.

'Ankles! It's ankles! No?'

As Hazel stepped out from behind a huge oak she finally caught a glimpse of the scene.

It was a monkey.

A talking monkey.

Oh dear.

It was quite large, with black fur, and it was crouching on its back legs like a person would. What on earth would a monkey be doing in the middle of the woods? Hazel felt pretty sure there weren't any monkeys in Britain. They lived in Africa, and South America, and India, and China, and lots of other places, but not Britain.

Hazel moved one foot forward as quietly as she could, and peered through the trees, squinting to see what was going on. She couldn't see who the monkey was talking to. How was it talking, anyway? Monkeys don't talk. Mind you, dogs don't have wooden heads either, but that didn't seem to bother anyone around here.

She inched her hand up to a branch, and moved it aside

in total silence, to get a good, clear look at the monkey. Aha! There it was.

But it wasn't a monkey.

It had a long, yellow tail with black spots, and where its monkey head should have been was the head of – a leopard!

It was like something out of a nightmare!

Hazel ducked back behind the oak. She couldn't have seen what she thought she saw, surely? She turned round to get a better look, quivering with fright. There it was, as clear as day. A monkey with a leopard's head. It had long, yellow fangs, and black lips, and flashing eyes. What was worse – it was even bigger than she first thought – not like a chimpanzee. Much more like . . . a gorilla! Half leopard, half gorilla! A gorilleopard! It was a monster! A monster! She must be dreaming!

Hazel tried very hard not to scream.

If she screamed, the gorilleopard would almost certainly come and eat her. As she bit her hand and shivered, the gorilleopard kept talking.

'This is ridiculous! We know that it's an object, and we know there's two words, and the first word is big. That could be anything! I give up. I'm fed up with this game. I'm going to bed.'

'Oh, come one! You've almost got it.'

This second voice came as if from nowhere, and was extremely high-pitched. Like a little elf, Hazel thought.

'Come on! You've almost got it.'

This didn't sound like the sort of conversation monsters should be having. Were they . . . playing charades?

'Oh, wait! Heel! You're pointing at my heel! Sounds like . . . wheel! A big wheel! Like at a circus!'

'Wait! . . . um . . . no . . . actually . . . that was too easy . . . can I change my mind?'

'What? No! You can't change to something else AFTER I've guessed what it is! I *hate* playing this game with you. This really is *it* – I'm going to bed.'

'GOT YOU!' Hazel felt herself being lifted, very suddenly, out of the bushes. She couldn't see what was lifting her, but it must have been very strong. It brought her straight into the clearing, and held her dangerously close to the fire. Whatever was she going to do now? The thing holding her spoke with an enormously deep, booming voice.

'LOOK WHO I FOUND SNEAKING AROUND.'

'It's the girl!' squeaked the tiny voice – though now she was in the clearing, Hazel still couldn't see where it came from.

'What? Oh, her. Well . . . I say we just throw her into the fire and be done with it. I'm really very tired now, and I won't be able to sleep with some little human child screaming all night.'

'WAIT — ARE YOU EATING MY BISCUITS AGAIN?'

The squeaky voice answered the REALLY big voice.

'Oh yes — sorry about that.'

'YOU DON'T HAVE TO STEAL MY BISCUITS. YOU DON'T EVEN LIKE BISCUITS.'

Hazel began to take in what she was seeing.

The REALLY big one, who was holding her above the fire, came into view as she spun slowly around in the air.

77

He wasn't holding her in his hand at all, but in his foot. He had the body and legs of an ostrich, but with claws so big and dexterous he could pick up a little girl with ease. He had no neck, and his face seemed to have been stuck straight onto his ostrich body. It was the face of a toad, with big, floppy lips, and slime all over it. You might have called it a frogstrich. It was tilted to the side as he lifted up his leg to show Hazel to the others.

And then she saw the other one. It was a great big snake. Well, almost. Because instead of a normal snake's head, it had the head of a sort of rodent, with great spiny needles, almost a foot long coming out of the back of its head – a porcupine! The spines ran most of the way down the creature's scaly back. It was half python, half porcupine – a pythupine! That's where the squeaky voice had been coming from.

'I think you two should shut up about the biscuits, kill the girl, and let me get some rest.'

'YOU HAVEN'T MOVED FROM THAT PATCH OF STRAW ALL DAY, GEOFF. WHAT DO YOU NEED REST FOR?'

Geoff? The gorilleopard was called Geoff?

'That question is so mind-blowingly stupid, Francis . . .'

Francis? The frogstrich was called Francis?

' . . . that I can't sum up the energy to answer it.'

Hazel thought it was about time she said something, in case she had to listen to this all night.

'Excuse me. My name's Hazel. I'm ten years old. Hello . . . um . . . what are your names?'

The monsters all looked at her, surprised. They didn't seem to know what to do. Then the pythupine spoke up.

'My name is Noel. This –' he indicated the gorilleopard

with his nose '– *is Geoff. And this is Francis.*'

Hazel summed up the courage to open her mouth again – something she was finding very hard to do without screaming.

'Well . . . I'm on holiday with Eugenia – who is my aunt – whilst my parents are in Egypt. What are you nice gentlemen doing here? On holiday as well?'

Hazel was trying very hard to pretend that nothing was wrong – just like she'd seen her parents do when something embarrassing or awkward happened – though she couldn't imagine what they'd do if they had these three come to dinner. She found the easiest way to pretend that everything was fine was to just imagine she was having a dream. A terrible dream that would be over as soon as she woke up.

Noel piped up.

'We're nightmares.'

Hazel blinked in disbelief. For a second she thought she'd actually been right – she'd just been having a dream. But then it occurred to her that the pythupine hadn't said she was IN a nightmare. He had said he *was* a nightmare. She hadn't realised nightmares lived in the woods.

Geoff groaned.

'If you two want a chit-chat with the child, then I'm going to bed.' He rolled over into the corner of the clearing and closed his eyes. Hazel tried to think what Mum and Dad would do.

'Oh! Nightmares! How interesting! Well . . . you certainly are very scary . . .'

Geoff roared from the corner.

'Yes we *are* very scary. In fact if you don't watch your

step we'll eat you. So there.'

'Yes — I suppose we will have to eat you if you cause us any trouble. So be careful.'

Hazel laughed nervously.

'Oh. Well. Fair enough, I guess.' Hazel smiled. 'What is it that nightmares do?'

'We scare Eugenia.'

Suddenly Hazel started to feel *very* curious.

'Scare Eugenia?'

'Yes. We're Eugenia's nightmares. It's our job to scare her. So we live in the woods, and every night we sneak into her room and frighten the living daylights out of her. As you can see — we're all extremely scary.'

Although they were very scary, Noel proudly squeaking about just how scary they were somehow made Hazel feel a bit less worried.

'CAN I PUT HER DOWN NOW?'

'I don't see why not. Put her down over here.'

Francis lumbered away from the fire, and put Hazel down on a log.

'DO YOU WANT SOME BISCUITS?'

'Hey! How come she gets biscuits and I don't?'

'YOU DIDN'T ASK. YOU JUST TOOK THEM. YOU HAVE TO ASK. IT'S JUST POLITE.'

Hazel held her breath and counted to ten very slowly. If she was going to get out of here alive, she was going to have to be very clever — which wasn't something she was normally very good at. Keeping one eye on Geoff, she tried to get more information.

'So what kind of things do you do to scare her?'

Noel looked very pleased to be asked.

'*Oh, you don't want to know. She hardly gets any sleep at all, you know. Too scared - too scared to sleep!*'

Hazel, though still scared, was thrilled. This was, quite simply, the best news she could possibly have received. There was a gang of monsters in the woods who spent every night tormenting horrible Aunt Eugenia. It was like Christmas, Easter, and Halloween all rolled into one. When she had first set out into the woods, she couldn't have hoped for a better result. Though still frightened, she was by now grinning from ear to ear.

'You must be very good at what you do. I was *petrified* when I first saw you all.' She didn't mention that she was still petrified.

'*Oh yes, we're as scary as anything you can imagine. In fact that's the whole point of being a nightmare. We're the scariest things imaginable. Otherwise we wouldn't be nightmares.*'

Hazel giggled.

'These biscuits are lovely, Francis.'

Francis smiled.

'THEY'VE GOT CINNAMON IN THEM.'

'Cinnamon? Oh, wow. That sounds good. What's cinnamon?'

Francis thought for a moment.

'I DON'T KNOW. GEOFF, DO YOU KONW WHAT CINNAMON IS?'

Geoff spun round grumpily.

'**I don't know, do I? Probably ground up babies' ears or something.**'

Hazel felt a little sick.

'*Francis? Can I have some if I promise not to steal any more?*'

'BUT YOU'VE ALREADY HAD LOADS.'

'*Oh please! I'm still hungry!*'

Hazel had an idea.

'I'm not hungry – you guys are so scary I've lost my appetite. Why don't you have some of mine, Noel?'

'*Really?*'

'Sure.'

Hazel thought that if Noel really wanted he could probably just poison her with his snake venom and take the biscuits.

'ALL I WANT IS FOR YOU TO ASK ME BEFORE YOU EAT THEM.'

Noel looked apologetic.

'*Sorry.*'

They seemed to have made peace. Hazel let her breath out, and put a finger in her ear to remove some of the sludge. Geoff seemed to be asleep by now, and Hazel definitely thought he was the scariest. With just Noel and Francis awake, she was as relaxed as she could be when talking to an eight-foot-tall half-frog half-ostrich nightmare, and a six-foot-long half-python half-porcupine nightmare.

As she handed him another biscuit, Noel grinned.

'*Thank you. That was kind of you.*'

Noel, who seemed to be, surprisingly, a rather friendly pythupine, slithered over and sat by Hazel.

Perhaps I should pause for one moment to make something clear. Hazel had no friends. None. What Noel had just said was the nicest thing anyone, excluding her parents, had ever said to her. It says something about the state of Hazel's social life that a half-python half-porcupine abomination whom she had only just met was the closest thing she had to a friend.

She felt herself starting to cry again – but stopped herself. She'd done quite enough crying since she got here. Besides, it looked like things might be starting to go her way.

'So . . . when's the next time you're going to scare Eugenia?'

'OH, WE WERE JUST ABOUT TO GO WHEN WE FINISHED OUR GAME OF CHARADES.'

'Really? You're doing a nightmare tonight?'

'*Yes. We do one every night.*'

Then, something very important happened. Noel seemed to have an idea.

'*Why don't you come with us?*'

Hazel had to fight very hard not to dance for joy.

The Sixth Chapter of this Book

From the Diary of Eugenia, Lady Pequierde:

We had grey skies for the sixth day in a row. Summer disappoints me again. Is it my imagination, or was summer once, a long time ago, much better? I am certain there were more butterflies. Why does everyone simply accept the poor quality of today's summers? Why is nothing done?

My wretched niece is still here.

Pude and Dungeon are thoroughly incompetent.

I am surrounded by morons.

I long for the earth to open up and swallow us all. What is that girl's name? She's called something ridiculous. Chestnut? What an awful, common little child she is.

I have decided to continue writing this diary, because my nightmares continue to haunt me. I would love to be able to simply finish my tea, brush my teeth, and slip off to bed – to enjoy a gentle, uninterrupted sleep. But instead I find myself sitting at my desk, describing the dream I had last night.

More than that, I describe this dream knowing that in an

hour or so, when I am in bed, the exact same dream will visit me again – as it has done every night for almost a year.

I do not know what I intend to gain by writing this diary.

How many times have I written that sentence? Hundreds, I suppose. Still, I do not know what I intend to gain. But I must do something. Something must be done.

Perhaps my niece's name is Coconut? I admit that seems unlikely. Wretched girl. The grotty thing stole my telephone the other day. Of course, I did my duty and disciplined her – I thought locking her in the greenhouse with all those flies would do the trick. However, I confess I haven't checked on her since. My nerves are shattered. I feel at my wit's end. Idiotic servants. No money. A barbarian at my dinner table. And still every night I return to my dream.

My dream was no different last night – it's coming is as certain as the moon, and the stars, and the lumpiness of Mrs Dungeon's gravy.

I closed my eyes, hoping I would be left alone just this once – hoping that I would be spared. But then I heard that breathing again.

Rattling, gurgling, inhuman breathing, came softly from the foot of my bed. I did not open my eyes, though I knew that soon I would be forced to. I began to hear the differences in the breathing. I felt certain that there were three people breathing in my room, but could not yet bear to open my eyes.

Then they began to sing.

Why do I think of it as singing? It is not singing. One voice hisses, like gas escaping from a pipe. One voice croaks, like a hundred doors to a hundred darkened rooms. And the last voice growls – low, and rough, and hateful.

It is not singing. But it seems to me as if I am being sung to by monsters – as if this was their idea of a lullaby.

I opened my eyes, and they stood before me – half-lit, shifting from side to side, and singing softly again.

I have described them before. I described them yesterday and I know that I will describe them tomorrow.

The first is a serpent. Its scales shine dim green under the light from the window. Its face is a rodent's face, with twitching whiskers. Long spines like knives run down its back.

The second is a sort of bird, but without wings or head, and on its body the dripping, stinking face of a toad. It stands eight feet tall, almost reaching the ceiling, and its eyes are pitch-black and wet.

The third, and most awful, is something between an ape and a leopard. Its tongue hangs out of its jaws, nestled between giant white fangs. Its tail whips swiftly behind it, and it rests a hand on my bed. The hand is almost like the hand of a man.

Those three monsters smelled foul in my dream, and I sat shivering in my bed, as they stared at me with monstrous eyes, and sang their terrible song. I woke up in a cold sweat the following morning, exhausted, as if I hadn't slept at all.

I never remember the end of the dream. It is as if the monsters stare at me for hours. They have stared at me for hours each night, month after month. I would rather not sleep at all.

Why do they torment me?

What have I done to deserve this?

Why will they not let me sleep?

I'm sure it'll be the same again tonight. Then I'll eat Mrs Dungeon's hideous lunch, and be forced to look at that vile girl, and drink tea, and eventually go to bed, and do it all over again.

Is the girl's name maybe Brazil?

* * *

Back at the campfire, Hazel was seeing what nightmares were really like.

'WOULD YOU LIKE A BISCUIT?'

'No, I'm fine thanks.'

'FAIR ENOUGH. THAT JUST LEAVES MORE BISCUITS FOR ME.'

Hazel thought that frightening Aunt Eugenia to within an inch of her life sounded like just about the best idea she had ever heard. Eugenia's usually cruel, rude, snobbish face being frozen in a mask of fear was a delicious treat to be enjoyed like ice-cream, or chocolate, or, in Mrs Dungeon's case, gravy.

But she had to be honest. The nightmare was RUB-BISH. R. U. B. B. I. S. H. Rubbish. They just stood there!

Hazel had watched the whole thing from the branch of a tree outside Eugenia's bedroom. She had seen the nightmares crawl up the wall and in through the window. She had seen Aunt Eugenia wake up. And she had seen them stand and stare at her. FOR HOURS.

Hazel thought that this was just about the worst nightmare she had ever seen.

She was still frightened of these monsters, if only because they could gobble her up without chewing if they wanted to. But now that she'd seen one of their nightmares, she knew that they needed her help. She had to say something, but she didn't know where to begin.

'So . . . um . . . that was a nightmare, huh?'

'It was indeed.'

Noel seemed very pleased with himself.

'Wow. Hmmm. So – is that pretty much what you normally do, or was it . . . a bit different tonight?'

Noel didn't understand. Francis was listening attentively, and Geoff was ignoring everyone.

'A bit different? No — it's like that every night.'

'Oh. Right. Every night?'

'Every night.'

Hazel scratched her head.

'So you just . . . sort of stand there and stare at her . . .'

' . . . and I hiss. And Francis croaks. And Geoff growls.'

'Oh. Yes. Of course. Do you stand in the same place every night?'

Hazel thought Noel was being very patient with her questions. He seemed, if anything, curious to know what she thought.

'Yes — I suppose we do.'

'Right. You never . . . get any closer to her?'

'OH, I COULDN'T!'

Francis suddenly appeared distressed.

' . . . um . . . why can't you get any closer to her?'

Francis looked very sorry for himself.

'I'M FRIGHTENED OF CUSHIONS.'

'Oh. Right. Um . . .'

Hazel was not impressed. Not impressed at all.

'Do you . . . um . . . do you do EXACTLY the same nightmare every night?'

Noel piped up cheerfully.

'Oh yes, it's exactly the same every night.'

Hazel felt very strongly that it was important to frighten Aunt Eugenia. She felt it was just about the most important thing she had to do right now. And if these monsters thought the best way to frighten Eugenia was to just stand there and stare at her, Hazel was going to have to talk them into doing something better.

'Well . . . I don't know anything, really . . . I mean I'm just a little girl. But, have you thought about . . . making the nightmare scarier?'

Noel pondered this.

'But, Hazel, I don't see how standing closer to her is going to make it scarier . . .'

'CAN WE PLEASE STOP TALKING ABOUT STANDING CLOSE TO HER!'

Francis stuffed about eight biscuits into his mouth, and glanced about anxiously.

This was going to take some doing to persuade them. They didn't look like very scary monsters at all, Hazel thought to herself. Noel was regarding himself in a little piece of broken mirror by the fire, Francis was stuffing his face, and Geoff was sullenly inspecting his belly-button.

'Well, it's not just where you're all standing in the room . . . although I'm sure you've thought very carefully about where to stand in the room . . . you could maybe . . . *do* some new things.'

They all looked deeply confused.

'DO YOU MEAN LIKE A SPECIAL DANCE?'

Noel became very excited.

'Oh, yes! A dance! Please let me do a dance! I'll scare the wits out of her with my incredible tap-dancing!'

The idea of a snake trying to tap-dance didn't strike Hazel as very scary.

'I meant more like, you know, scary things.'

Another confused silence.

'YOU MEAN CUSHIONS, RIGHT?'

' . . . No. Not cushions . . . um . . .'

'Maybe if we all went in there and gave her the silent treatment? Just ignored her.' Noel seemed to find this idea very frightening indeed.

'WHAT ABOUT A SOFA? I CAN'T THINK OF ANYTHING MORE FRIGHTENING THAN A SOFA.'

Geoff spoke up from his corner.

'She's means SCARY, you idiots, not vaguely annoying. Like tearing off her face, or cooking her in a big pot.'

Hazel felt a little sick again.

'No! I don't mean tearing off her face! She wouldn't have time to be scared whilst she was dying horribly of facelessness! I mean something . . . subtle.'

Geoff thought for a second.

'Peeling her face off slowly, you mean?'

'Forget about her face!'

Geoff sat up ever so slightly and growled.

'Do NOT speak to me like that, little girl.'

Hazel held her breath.

'Geoff, don't scare her,' said Noel softly.

Hazel suddenly became very excited.

'That's it! Scary! Scary! It's subtle. Sometimes just little things are scary. Like you feel about cushions, Francis . . .'

'OH, DON'T BE SURE. SOME CUSHIONS AREN'T LITTLE AT ALL. SOME ARE HUGE.'

Francis looked very worried. Noel gave him a friendly pat on the leg.

Hazel got very excited about that look being on Aunt Eugenia's face. Real fear.

Noel was starting to understand.

'So we need to think what little things scare her, to make something more subtle?'

'Yes.'

Noel looked gleeful.

'Oh, Hazel, this is wonderful! You're right, we can make these nightmares much better. You're so clever! You must be our director!'

Hazel felt all warm inside. Noel really wanted her to help out.

'Well, we'll see what we can do.'

Geoff did not look impressed.

'What a lot of nonsense.'

'Oh please, Geoff, please help out, this new nightmare will be brilliant, I'm sure', said Noel.

Geoff didn't look so keen, and Francis was still having a hard time thinking about the cushions, but Noel was clearly desperate to make a new nightmare.

'I think we should let Hazel be our director! She's right. The nightmares haven't been any good for ages. With her new ideas, we can do something really horrific. Agreed?'

Francis smiled.

'YEAH. OK.'

Geoff grimaced and said nothing.

At this point, Hazel, having promised herself she wouldn't cry, burst into tears.

She had made some friends.

The Seventh Chapter of this Book

Hazel awoke feeling ten times better. She'd only had a few hours' sleep, and it was already noon — but nothing happened in the house before then anyway, other than Isambard feeding his pets. She stretched her arms and yawned, thinking happily about her new friends.

The clouds had cleared a little today, and the ice-cold room had begun to heat up in the sun. Hazel hopped out of bed, put on her jeans and T-shirt, and prepared herself for a difficult lunch with Eugenia.

She shut the door of her room, and skipped off to the staircase — but was stopped in her tracks by loud voices from down below.

Eugenia was obviously in a bad mood.

'What is this? What *is* this? Are you all *insane*? What am I supposed to *do* with it?'

'Well, ma'am . . .'

'Shut up! Did I ask you a question?'

'. . . um . . .'

'Well, shut up then!'

Hazel crept down the first flight of stairs, and poked her head around the banister. At the bottom of the stairs were Eugenia, Pude, Dungeon, and a man who was surely Boynce the gardener. He held a weather-beaten old hat tightly in his hands, and was a bit younger than Eugenia, with curly blond hair and rosy cheeks.

'Of all the lazy, ridiculous, half-baked, cockamamie ideas anyone has ever thought of, this is the very worst. I mean, look at the wretched thing!'

Sat in the midst of them, shivering and bleating, was a baby goat. It was snowy white, with a pink mouth, and it hadn't any horns yet.

'Meeargh!'

'Oh *do* shut this appalling creature up!'

The goat was quite unaware of what was going on around it, and seemed mostly concerned with getting some food. Eugenia paced up and down, never taking her eyes off the three culprits.

'He's only little, ma'am. He's cryin' for a bit of milk,' said Boynce, in a gentle, mellifluous voice.

'What?! Goats don't drink milk, they produce it, you oaf. Don't you know anything? What do you *do* all day in the fields that you think goats drink milk? Twiddle your thumbs?'

Boynce looked confused.

'But, ma'am – the mummy goat makes the milk so the baby goat can drink it . . .'

'I'm the one who drinks the milk, Boynce, on the rare

occasions when these two imbeciles see fit to bring me my tea!'

Pude coughed, and joined in.

'Well, ma'am, it wasn't so much for milk that we got it — we got it cos, well, we thought it was a sweet little thing, and it might cheer you up a bit.' Pude looked very awkward, but decided to go on. 'What with your moods an' all.'

At this, Eugenia came right up to Pude's face and hissed at him, 'What do you *mean* my moods?'

Pude coughed again.

'Well, you know, you've been a bit down in the dumps is all. We saw this cute little fella down at Boynce's brother's dairy farm an' thought he might bring a bit o' sunshine into your life.'

Eugenia was not giving up.

'You didn't answer my question, *Pude*. What do you *mean* my moods?'

Pude looked desperately to Boynce and Dungeon, but they didn't seem to have any answers.

'Well, you can be a bit, well . . . foul-tempered.'

Eugenia was perfectly still.

'Meeargh?'

She spun round, kicked the goat, and turned back to Pude. The goat scrabbled to the far corner of the hall and hid behind a pile of magazines.

'Foul, am I?'

Pude was beside himself.

'No! No, that's not what I meant . . .'

'You know what's foul, *Pude*? What's foul is the stench

of people so gob-smackingly dim-witted that they think the way to cheer me up is to deposit an as-yet-un-house-trained goat in my hallway. What's foul is the smell of your slowly rotting brain, festering in its juices, farting gaseously stupid ideas out of your mouth and into the atmosphere. What is *foul*, is *you*.'

Eugenia stood back from Pude, triumphant.

'Now I want you to shut up, drown this vermin in the lake, and get about your duties.'

This was too much for Mrs Dungeon.

'Oh, please, ma'am, we won't bother you with it any more – we just thought you might like it! It's done nothin' to you! We'll just take it back to the farm an' say no more about it.'

'WHETHER you *do* or *do not* say any more about it, is not a subject for negotiation, Mrs Dungeon. You will absolutely never, under any circumstances, mention this debacle again. More than that, you will drown this goat.'

Mrs Dungeon gasped.

'Please, ma'am – don't be so cruel.'

Eugenia would not be reasoned with.

'You know who's cruel, Mrs Dungeon? Do you really want to know who? Not me, that's for certain. I am only a poor woman trying to remove a goat from her family home. The cruel ones are your parents. Your parents committed a quite unforgivable act of cruelty when they failed to strangle you in your cot. They quite callously let loose upon the world a woman so ignorant, fat, ugly, and disorientatingly gravy-obsessed that anyone who encounters her feels wretched for weeks afterwards.'

Eugenia marched into her drawing room and slammed the door shut.

Pude put an arm around the distraught Mrs Dungeon, and Boynce padded softly over to the corner to extract the goat from the magazines.

'There, there, Mrs Dungeon', said Pude.

'There, there, Gunther,' said Boynce.

'It's not *fair*. The poor little creature never did nothin'. Never had *time* to do nothin'. And now he's only going to get thrown in a lake!'

Pude frowned.

'Our plan for cheerin' her up certainly did backfire, didn't it?'

Boynce had managed to get the goat out of the corner and under his coat.

'Well — I don't see that we have to throw it in the lake. She'll never know.'

Dungeon brightened up, and Pude gave Boynce a little thumbs-up.

'Good idea, Boynce. She needn't know.'

Dungeon suddenly started to look sad again.

'She said I was ugly.'

Pude and Boynce both came over to give her a hug. Pude frowned again.

'We shouldn't stand for it, you know — the things we let her get away with!'

They grumbled quietly, and, resigning themselves to what had happened, went off to get about their day. Was there *anyone* Eugenia was nice to?

* * *

Hazel pulled a chair out from the table, and sat to wait for her lunch. It didn't look like anyone was going to be joining her, until she heard a cough behind her.

She turned and saw Isambard standing by the door, scratching his head anxiously.

'Hi,' she said, and turned back to the table. She didn't feel like talking to him.

Isambard huffed, and scrambled quickly over to his place. He got up on his chair, and looked at Hazel, who was not looking back at him. He frowned, thinking what to do. Then, struck by an idea, he got down, went to the middle of the long, old table, and picked up a pot of salt. He brought it over to Hazel.

'Would you like some salt?'

'No, I would *not* like some salt, thank you. I don't even have any food to put it on.'

'Oh . . . sure.'

Isambard wandered back to his seat, muttering to himself, 'stupid, stupid, stupid'.

He stared out the window, and then looked back to her.

'You didn't feel like feeding the pets this morning?'

'No.'

'Oh. That's a pity. It was really fun.' Isambard didn't look like it had been any fun at all.

He was being *so* annoying.

Swinging his legs back and forth under his chair, no idea what to do, he dipped his hand into the salt, and put a big lump in his mouth. He looked surprised, and then began to retch.

'Aak! . . . aak . . . nnng!'

Hazel groaned.

'Oh, for heaven's sake – what are you *doing?*'

She brought the glass of water at her place over to him, and held his head while he drank it. He gulped gratefully. He spluttered and coughed a little more, and then was silent. Hazel went back to her seat. Isambard was bright red with embarrassment.

'Hazel?'

'What?'

' . . . Can I talk to you?'

'You're talking to me right now.'

Isambard looked at her wide-eyed, and muttered again under his breath, 'stupid, stupid, stupid'.

'Well – I wanted to say sorry.'

Though Hazel was surprised by the apology, she certainly didn't think it was good enough.

'Well then *say* sorry!'

Nothing is worse than a botched apology, reader, remember that. There was once a writer who was writing a book about ancient Rome, and accidentally put the hero in the path of an oncoming chariot. Terrible mess. Blood everywhere. What's more, it was only halfway through the book, and he had no idea what to do with the next two hundred pages. So, in an effort to make up for his mistake, rather than simply apologising and ending the book there and then, he told a story about a lovely pixie making a bunch of flowers for her best friend. It went on for hundreds of pages, and had nothing whatsoever to do with all the stuff set in Rome. He spent sixteen pages describing a daisy. It was awful. Of course, he'd only made things worse. All people want is a simple apology – don't make it all about you and how bad *you* feel, and if you're going to give them a gift make sure it's a gift the person wants, rather than a pot of salt or a two-hundred-page story about a pixie. And don't forget to actually *say* sorry.

'Sorry. I'm really sorry. I wanted to . . . I'm just . . . I'm so scared of her . . . please . . . um . . .'

Isambard couldn't go on. He stared down at the ground for a moment, and then ran out of the room.

She was glad he said sorry, but she was still disappointed in him – he'd completely let her down, and he'd need to do much better than this to win back her good opinion. Dungeon came through the door carrying two plates of steaming cabbage.

'Oh – where's Master Isambard, dear?'

'He's not having lunch, I don't think.'

Hazel felt bad as she finished her meal alone.

After lunch, Hazel went up to her room for a bit of a think. She was trying to come up with a good nightmare for tonight, but she found herself having another thought. If she could persuade the monsters to do something about Eugenia – maybe she could persuade Dungeon, Pude and Boynce as well. It was an unusual feeling for Hazel – the feeling that she could do something. But it had worked last time, so why not give it a try?

She left her room to head downstairs. After a quick search, she heard voices outside. On the side of the house was a little back door to the kitchen, and at it stood Boynce with a big sack of grey, sorry-looking potatoes. Hazel shuddered. She would presumably be eating them later.

Pude and Dungeon were standing chatting with Boynce.

'Excuse me,' she said, trotting over from where she'd been watching, 'hi!'

'Oh, hello, little girl – what have you come looking for?' said Pude warmly.

Hazel didn't know how best to put it.

'Well – I heard the whole thing with the goat . . . you know . . . and you saying about how much you let Eugenia get away with.'

They all looked nervous – Pude in particular became very flustered.

'No! Oh, you must have misheard us! We . . . um . . . we love working for Lady Pequierde. She's . . . firm but fair?'

He wasn't even convincing himself.

'You don't have to pretend – it's all right,' now Hazel whispered. 'I think she's *horrible*.'

Hazel giggled. Then Dungeon, then Boynce, then Pude.

'She says horrible things to me too – all the time! She's never nice to anyone.'

Boynce chuckled warmly.

'No, miss, you're right, she certainly isn't. One time she told me to go and throw myself in the fire for being so stupid. Fancy that! I hadn't even done anything.'

Pude joined in.

'Once, I bought a new stereo for listening to music and so on – she got so annoyed! She screamed at me an' told me to smash it up with a hammer or I weren't getting no pay that month! I had to do it, didn't I? Wallop! Poor old stereo!'

They all began to laugh. Pude, worried that Eugenia might hear, held his finger up to his lips, and nodded to the kitchen. They all shuffled in, and had a good old guffaw.

'She can be terrible — I didn't do nothing to deserve being called ugly and fat and what not,' Dungeon sighed. 'Well, what goes around comes around. I'm sure she'll get her comeuppance one of these days.'

Hazel realised this was the moment at which to say something.

'Maybe she could get her comeuppance today?'

They all looked at her, quite surprised.

'Whatever do you mean?' said Boynce.

'Well — maybe we could do something to get back at her. Something small. Something she'd barely notice. I don't know what.'

Hazel really didn't know what. She was hoping they might have some suggestions. Pude harrumphed.

'Oh, I don't know — best to let sleeping dogs lie, I say. She'll calm down one of these days.'

Boynce nodded.

'She didn't even win this one — I'll just go and hide Gunther, and it'll all be back to normal.'

Then Dungeon, who had been most hurt by Eugenia's latest outburst, spoke up.

'We could put socks in her tea.'

Pude and Boynce looked very surprised to see nice Mrs Dungeon say something like this.

'We just need to boil old socks in the water, and it'll leave a faint smell — but a horrid one. It'll be like someone's farted, but she won't know who.' She seemed very pleased with herself, but Pude looked doubtful and so did Boynce.

'I don't know . . .'

'Imagine the look on her face.'

Hazel was surprised to see the fire in Mrs Dungeon's eyes when she said this. After years of abuse, she had finally been pushed too far. With that delicious thought of revenge, Pude and Boynce smiled, and nodded silently in agreement.

Things were starting to turn in Hazel's favour. She was uplifted to see people finally becoming brave in this house. As Pude, Boynce, and Dungeon shuffled off to get on with their day, Hazel hummed a little tune to herself, and skipped outside, thinking about what she was going to do to scare Eugenia that night.

The Eighth Chapter of this Book

From the Diary of Lady Eugenia Pequierde

This will be the strangest diary entry I have written in a year.

I almost cannot believe I am writing it.

I went to bed as usual last night – a little tea, a wash, wrote up the nightmare from the night before and prepared myself for the next one. Little did I know what was about to happen.

I suppose I should make some record of the rest of my day. Hazel continues to appal me. My servants brought a goat into my home for no sensible reason, and I considered having them flogged, but in the end decided against it. Tea was, as usual, dreadful.

Now on to my nightmare.

As usual I closed my eyes and drifted off to sleep. I found myself in my room, just as I always do, waiting to hear those terrible monsters. I kept my eyes closed and hoped they would not come.

And they didn't!

After what must have been half an hour of waiting in silent dread, I opened my eyes and looked about. I was alone! I must record that I was quite petrified. Why had they not come? Were they waiting for me to come to the window? Were they under my bed?

Very slowly, I peered over the edge of the duvet. It was, of course, very dark under my bed- but there didn't seem to be any monsters. I was going out of my mind – WHERE WERE THEY?

But then, all of a sudden, one of them rushed in – the serpent.

I cowered against the pillow as it slithered through the window, across my floor, and over the sheets of my bed – where it held its ghastly face before mine and shrieked.

I do not remember precisely what it said, but it was something along the lines of –

'Who's the most frightening? Who's the most frightening?! I'll crawl up your face and tickle your eyes! I'll crawl through your ear and eat your brain! I'll crawl down your throat and make a nest in your heart! I am the best! I am the best! Say I'm the most frightening! Yes! Yes! Be afraid! Sweat! Shiver! Cry!'

I was, of course, quite terrified.

After that, the monstrosity left me, and I woke up to my cold sweat. But I must admit that in a way I was relieved. I have been having the same nightmare for a year, and the serpent's strange speech was, at least, a change. For that I am grateful. Though I was scared, it was better to at least have some variety.

I am filled with curiosity as I go to bed now. Will tonight's nightmare be different as well? What do my dreams hold in store for me?

There is, I suppose, only one way to find out.

What was that!? What were you doing!? Why did you . . .
how did you . . . when did you . . . *Noel!'*

Hazel was furious.

They were back in the woods now, and Noel was looking very sorry for himself. Francis sat beside him, equally
embarrassed, while Hazel ranted in front of them. Geoff
lay on the other side of the fire, unconcerned.

Geoff had flatly refused to join in the nightmare, insisting that he just couldn't be bothered. Whilst Hazel had
gone with Noel and Francis to Eugenia's room, he had
simply stayed behind and slept.

'We were supposed to wait as long as possible before
crawling in, and you just . . . you just . . . what was that
speech? What was all that stuff about crawling into her
brain? I'm not sure that's even possible!'

Hazel was jumping up and down now, not even looking
at Noel, and finding it difficult to explain just how
immensely, enormously, head-explodingly angry she was.
She'd come up with a brand-new, much better idea for a
dream, and Noel had completely ruined it.

'Its just . . . it's just . . . I mean . . . aargh!'

Francis and Noel didn't know what to do.

Francis tried to be helpful.

'WELL, I THOUGHT IT WAS QUITE SCARY. WHEN NOEL
WAS SAYING HIS . . . UM . . . SPEECH, EUGENIA LOOKED
REALLY CONFUSED.'

This made Hazel even angrier.

'That's not being frightened! That's just being annoyed!

I'm trying to make that horrible woman scared! Not irritated! I want her to wet herself in terror, not cover her ears!'

Hazel fell silent, and sat down on the twigs at her feet. She was thinking very hard.

Noel chose this moment to explain himself.

'I know now that what I did was wrong. I'm SO sorry. Please, please, PLEASE accept my sincerest apologies. You see, when I think about myself, I think one of the main things about me is that I . . .'

Francis nudged him and gave him a look that said 'NOT NOW.'

'Well, maybe you should punish me?'

'NOEL, WE'RE NOT GOING TO PUNISH YOU. YOU JUST WANT TO TALK ABOUT YOURSELF AGAIN . . .'

'Do you think so? Really? What is it about me that makes me want to talk about myself, do you think? Is it something that happened in my childhood?'

'OH SHUT UP AND HAVE A BISCUIT.'

The nightmares were clearly going to need a lot more work. But it was almost morning, and it was time for Hazel to get back to the house for a few hours' sleep. As she began to head back, Francis and Noel were still sitting glumly in silence. Good. She would leave them to think about what they had done.

* * *

Hazel awoke in a bad mood. A mood made worse by knowing that Eugenia was probably waking up having had a comfortable night's sleep.

It was noon. She threw on her clothes and dragged her feet all the way down the stairs to lunch, yawning loudly.

Isambard was already at the table.

'Oh . . . hi,' she said.

Isambard looked up and smiled. Then, embarrassed, returned to his sprouts.

Hazel took up her place opposite him, and said nothing. It looked like being another uncomfortable lunch. Mrs Dungeon arrived with Hazel's plate, and gave her a conspiratorial wink. This cheered Hazel up – she assumed it meant that Mrs Dungeon had started putting socks in Eugenia's tea. Which was something, at least.

Hazel played with her food and made long, low, snorting sounds – which was something she did when she was angry. Isambard looked alarmed.

' . . . Ah . . . cousin . . . are you OK?'

Hazel put down her fork.

'Yes. I'm OK.'

She picked up her fork and began to play with her food again.

' . . . Because you don't look OK.'

She put down her fork again

'Well I *am*.'

Isambard took a deep breath.

'I hope it's not because of me.'

He did seem to be trying. Hazel gave him a weak little smile.

'No. It's fine.'

Isambard would not be put off. He reached for the pot of salt, thought better of it, and then got out of his chair.

He was now standing beside her.

'Hazel – you're a clever girl . . .'

Hazel was stunned. Still holding her fork in her hand, and with a mouthful of sprouts, she turned to look at him.

' . . . and I need someone clever to help me with something.'

He stopped here, a little surprised at how confident he was being. He scratched his head, and decided to go on.

'You see, I've written . . . um . . . a play . . .'

But somehow the word 'play' completely sunk him, like a well-aimed rock at a paper boat. He stared at the ground, coughed, scratched his head, and returned to his seat. Not looking at Hazel, he ate his sprouts, as if nothing had happened.

Hazel swallowed her mouthful.

' . . . What's the play about?'

'Well! I'm glad you asked. It's about . . . um . . . this boy.'

He fell silent again.

' . . . and?'

' . . . and what?'

Hazel put down her fork again.

'Is it about anything else other than a boy? I mean what does he do?'

Isambard took a deep breath.

'Well — he has a mother.'

Silence.

'OK. Most boys have mothers, don't they? Does anything else happen?'

Isambard looked like he might run away again.

'Well. He . . . he stands up to her. You know.'

He stared at his plate and began furiously to devour his sprouts.

Poor old Isambard. Hazel could see that, in his own way, he was trying to be brave. She got off her chair, and went over.

'Can I read it?'

His eyes lit up.

'Sure!'

'You know – if you wanted, we could act it out.'

'Really?'

'Yeah. We could perform it for Mrs Dungeon, and Pude, and maybe Boynce if he has time.'

Isambard was discouraged.

'Oh, I don't think I'd want to do that. I'd be very scared of acting it out for others to watch. Besides, there are three parts, and only two of us.'

'Oh. Well – how about I get Boynce, Dungeon and Pude to act it out for you? I'm sure they'd be happy to. I'll direct them. It'll take . . . maybe a week? We can perform it next Saturday morning.'

Hazel thought it would be a bit like the nightmares, and couldn't be much harder than directing an eight-foot frogstrich.

'Really? Would you do that?'

'Sure. If you give me the play, I'll do some rehearsals with them.'

Isambard jumped down and gave her hug. This was unexpected. Hazel awkwardly hugged him back.

Then Isambard ran away – straight out the door.

'Isambard!'

That boy was impossible. Where had he gone?

A moment later, Hazel found out, as Isambard sprinted

back into the room, clutching a handful of crumpled paper.

'There's only one copy. Sorry.'

He gave her another hug, and ran away again.

Hazel looked at the pages. They were the crumpled evidence of Isambard's courage. She promised herself that she would do a good job of directing his play.

All of a sudden, she realised she wasn't worried about what to do for the next two weeks. She was worried about how she was going to have time to do it all. Which was better by far, she thought.

The Ninth Chapter

of this Book

Hazel began to settle into a kind of routine. Wake up, eat lunch, try to get people to rehearse Isambard's play, fail, plan a nightmare, eat dinner, go back to her room for more planning, head out to the woods when night fell, tell Francis and Noel what they were doing, go to Eugenia's room to do the nightmare, go to the camp to talk about it, go home near dawn, get a few hours' sleep and start all over again.

She didn't see much of her aunt as the days went by. Eugenia got up late, took her meals in the drawing room, and occasionally could be heard gagging at the foul tea she was being served. In fact, Hazel saw more of her after dark.

She sat in the tree opposite the window every night, whilst Francis and Noel carried out her orders in the bedroom. She'd watch, and listen to hear if Eugenia screamed – which she never did – or if Noel did his speech again – which thankfully he didn't.

After the nightmare, she would take notes while they told her how it went. She wanted to know which bits Eugenia looked scared by, and which bits Francis and Noel found difficult. Geoff was rarely seen, and when he did appear by the fire, it was only to sleep. She didn't know what he was up to alone in the woods, and she wasn't sure she wanted to know. He seemed a different sort of creature to Francis and Noel, and she had to admit she was still scared of him.

Dungeon could be heard chuckling away to herself in the kitchen while she boiled the socks. She only did it to some of the mugs of tea, so Eugenia could never be sure whether she'd get the horrid smell or not. Pude would get very worried about being caught, but Eugenia never seemed to catch on.

Whenever she found time, Hazel would beg people to rehearse Isambard's play. She managed to get an hour or two in, but what with the busy days everybody worked, and all the time Hazel spent thinking about and planning the nightmares, she worried whether she'd ever finish it.

Isambard was reclusive. He spent most of the day up in his room revising, and Hazel never disturbed him from it. They'd have lunch and dinner together, and Isambard would make awkward jokes, and be far too shy to ask how the play was going. He just trusted that eventually Hazel would get round to showing it to him.

The nightmares were the main thing, though. They were what consumed Hazel's thoughts. Every morning, she told herself that tonight would be the night. Tonight she would show her. Tonight she would get a full-throated scream out of Eugenia, Lady Pequierde.

* * *

From the diary of Eugenia, Lady Pequierde:

. . . Last night the dream was different again. I awoke to an empty room, with the monsters nowhere in sight, but after a few moments became aware that the breathing was there – very soft – and I realised with horror that it came from beneath my bed. I was ready to die of fright, when the bird-monster suddenly leapt out from under the bed and bolted to the window. The serpent followed a moment later, and I was unexpectedly left in peace . . .

Poor Francis had been unable to deal with being so close to the cushions, and had fled the room to hide up a tree. It took two hours and an enormous plate of biscuits to coax him down.

On this night I again could not see the monsters. Instead, I heard a low, painful moaning, from just outside my window. It was as if two creatures were being tortured. But then, only a short while after it began, it ended, and my nightmare was over . . .

After about half an hour of energetic moaning, Francis's throat was dry and cracked, and Noel had totally lost his voice.

. . . I felt my bed begin to shake, terribly, as if a monster were beneath it again. I was afraid at first, but soon the shaking stopped, and I heard what sounded like a sort of exhausted panting – and the nightmare was over . . .

115

The idea had been to create a sort of earthquake effect, but with Francis too frightened to go under the bed, Noel had to do it on his own – and he got tired after about ten minutes.

. . . I beheld the awful creatures again, but this time the half-leopard thing was missing, and the other two awoke me with dancing. The dancing was very strange and inhuman, but also somewhat foolish, and, to be frank, I laughed heartily . . .

Well *obviously* a scary dance was never going to work.

. . . This dream was the strangest yet. I awoke to a heap of cushions (I recognised some from my drawing room) being flung at me from the window. Being cushions they did not hurt a great deal, and after a little while it stopped anyway . . .

This was Francis's idea, and although Eugenia wasn't frightened, he went straight back up his tree muttering 'THE CUSHIONS . . . THE CUSHIONS . . . SO MANY . . . SO MANY', so at least he'd done a good job of scaring himself.

. . . I was disturbed tonight by a strange sequence of words and phrases, muttered by the monsters from the darkness. They said things such as 'SEVENTEEN', 'forty-one', 'NINE', 'blatantly', 'LETTUCE', 'Nottingham', 'EIGHTY-FIVE', 'moisturiser', 'OLD RED EYES IS BACK', 'disco', 'TWELVE', 'six', 'JUG', 'Tom Cruise'. I can't say I was even slightly scared. Things are looking up . . .

Well, the idea of that one was to say strange things to 'confuse' Eugenia – but if Hazel was honest she had just run out of ideas.

. . . The creatures attacked me with childish insults from the bottom of my bed. They called me 'old' and 'ugly'. I am glad to say I responded by telling the beasts exactly what I thought of THEM . . .

'The things she said . . . no one's ever said anything that mean to me! Not even Geoff!'

'SHE SAID MY VOICE SOUNDED LIKE I'D BEEN HIT ON THE HEAD WITH A CRICKET BAT! DOES MY VOICE SOUND LIKE THAT?'

' . . . who does she think she is?! I do not sound like an elf!'

' . . . I SUPPOSE OUR INSULTS WEREN'T VERY GOOD, BUT SHE DIDN'T HAVE TO BE THAT MEAN. I DON'T SMELL, ANYWAY. DO I?'

' . . . I'd like to tell her a thing or two about dancing! I've got amazing footwork! What does she know?'

By the time they got back to the camp, they were exhausted and dejected.

The nightmares were getting them nowhere – but Hazel saw that Noel and Francis had really tried. She asked them to do completely different things to what they were used to, and they just did the best they could.

It was clearly starting to get them down.

Francis was eating more and more biscuits, and even seemed to be putting on weight. Noel nervously chewed his tail, and was always asking if Hazel thought he'd been scary that night.

It occurred to Hazel that she'd been asking a lot of them. She remembered how sad Noel looked after she shouted at him for his speech.

She sat herself down on a log, and looked at her monsters. Francis was fiddling with a biscuit wrapper, mumbling to himself. Noel was sitting very still, looking at himself in his little piece of mirror, with a pained expression on his face. Geoff was nowhere to be seen.

She summoned up her strength, and prepared to do something she had never done before. She wasn't very good at knowing what to do when someone is upset. Somehow she didn't feel able to hug them, like her parents would have done. They were monsters after all – but still, she wished she could.

'Guys? How are you feeling?'

Francis left his biscuits, and looked to Noel for help. Noel took it upon himself to speak for both of them.

'We feel like a useless pair of freaks.'

Hazel gulped. That was something she had been called. That summer term, playing netball at school, she'd dropped the ball in a particularly lame way, and a girl had called her that. A useless freak. It wasn't a nice thing to feel like you were.

'I don't think you're a freak – I think you're lovely.'

Noel turned away from his mirror. He was very still.

'Am I? Am I lovely?'

Hazel took a deep breath.

'Yes – you're lovely, Noel.'

'AND WHAT ABOUT ME? AM I LOVELY?'

'Yes! You are lovely, Francis.'

'OH, THANK YOU!'

'You're welcome. I just want to tell you both what a good job I think you've been doing. I know it's not . . . um . . . been going so well . . . but you've both been . . . you know. Brilliant. And I'm sorry for shouting.'

At this point, Hazel ran out of things to say. There was silence. Then Francis stood up, hopped over to her, and placed a single biscuit in her hand. He smiled, and sat down beside her. Then Noel skittered over and curled up at her feet.

Hazel had a very happy sort of feeling in her toes. She reached out her hand, and gave Francis an affectionate pat on the head.

There they sat, three freaks in the forest, eating their biscuits, until it was time for Hazel to go.

* * *

Hazel made her way back to the house at dawn, sneaked in through the kitchen and up the stairs to bed.

However, that night, something disturbed her journey back. She could hear creaking floorboards above her. Having had pretty much the bravest week of her whole life, she decided now was no time to chicken out. She dropped off her boots and notepad in her room, and tip-toed up the stairs to the top floor.

This was the attic, where Isambard lived. She'd never wanted to disturb him before, so it was a new world to her.

The paint on the walls was even more decayed than in the rest of the house, and there were no portraits. The ceiling seemed lower here, and it occurred to Hazel that in the old days the top floor was where the servants lived, and their rooms would have been smaller. Why would Isambard want to live up in a small room?

A low dawn light was beginning to seep in through a small window at the east end of the corridor. Hazel waited, very still. The corridor was empty, but she was sure she had heard floorboards creaking. She pressed up against the wall, hiding in the shadows.

There it was again! At the west end of the long passage-way, from behind one of the doors. She inched towards the sound. As she brushed past the wall, she knocked a cloud of dust into the air. She held her nose, desperately trying not to cough. How could Isambard live up here? It was a barren, unwelcoming place, with no paintings, or pretty colours, or even the piles of magazines and crockery found in the drawing room. It was as if Eugenia had deliberately put him away in the attic – like a piece of furniture she didn't like to look at too often.

The creaking was definitely coming from the last door on the left. There were fewer spider webs in this corner – suggesting the door was opened and closed regularly. The door, Hazel guessed, must lead up to one of the four tow-ers. She hadn't realised Isambard lived in a tower! She'd thought he lived in one of these rooms off the corridor. It occurred to Hazel that if you had a mother like Eugenia, being able to retreat up to your own private tower to escape from her would be pretty much ideal. It must have been nice for him to be able to look out of the window so high up, and see his dog in the kennel, and his pigs in their pen, and his ducks on the lake.

She wondered if she should open the door? Maybe it was just Isambard getting up in the middle of the night to . . . get a glass of water? She'd never heard him getting up in the middle of the night before.

Suddenly Hazel's heart sank, as the door began to open, very slowly. She looked around for somewhere to hide, but she would make far too much noise opening another door to hide behind. As her heart raced, she tried to reassure herself that it was Isambard, and that he'd be perfectly friendly.

But it wasn't Isambard — it was someone very tall, and very broad.

Hazel held her breath.

Geoff's massive head emerged from out of the tower. He sniffed the air once, twice, and leaped round the door to pick Hazel up by the collar of her T-shirt.

'Eeeek!'

Hazel's mind was racing — what was Geoff doing here? Why was he sneaking about in the house? Had he been giving Isambard a nightmare?

'Geoff . . . what . . . what are you doing here?'

Geoff glared at her with those yellow eyes, and growled.

' . . . Are you . . . um . . . what have you done to Isambard?'

If Geoff had wanted, he could easily have thrown Hazel out the window, or worse. Hazel felt quite ill as it occurred to her that Geoff could easily fit her whole head in his mouth.

'I'm just . . . you know . . .'

He suddenly seemed very angry. He dropped Hazel on the ground, and turned swiftly to the window. As he began to open it, Hazel caught a glance into the tower's steps. There, very old and battered-looking, stood a boot.

He was just about to leap out on to the roof, when Hazel, not thinking what she was doing, or how Geoff might react, yelped, 'What's that boot doing there?'

He paused, uncertain what to do.

'It's . . . it's . . . never mind . . . you never saw anything, understand?'

He glared at her. He obviously didn't want her to know about it. Hazel had a rather brave, mischievous thought.

'Well, I'm sure I can just ask Isambard what it is. Don't worry about it. I'll chat to him in the morning.'

Geoff looked enraged.

'No! You mustn't . . . don't ask him . . .'

'I think maybe I *will* ask him.' Hazel was finding it hard to believe how brave she was being.

'No! Don't . . . it's . . . it's . . . ' Geoff groaned, and his shoulders sagged. **'Look — you mustn't tell anyone. It's just a little present for the boy. All right?'**

A present?

'A present?'

'*Yes*, a *present*. I just thought the boy could do with some cheering up.'

This was one of the most confusing things that had happened in the house so far, thought Hazel. And that was saying something.

'Right. So . . . it's a present. Right. Why did you get him a boot for a present?'

Geoff growled so loudly Hazel thought Isambard might wake up.

'It's not just a *boot*!'

Then, quite unexpectedly, a soft, kind look passed over Geoff's gruesome face. A look that was something like pity.

'It's his father's boot.' Geoff paused, and took a deep breath. **'I heard the boy say his father, when he was alive, lost his boot in the woods when he was out riding one day. He lost control of his horse and . . . I've been looking for it.'**

Hazel was stunned.

'So that's what you've been doing all this time?'

'**Well, I didn't know what his father** *smelled* **like, so** *yes*, **it took me a while!**'

Geoff looked towards the boot forlornly. Hazel laughed.

'**What are you laughing at!**'

'Ha ha! Oh, Geoff, you're just a big softie – you're just a pussy-cat!'

Geoff looked mortified.

'**You mustn't tell anyone about this!**'

Hazel smiled.

'Oh, but maybe I will tell someone about this – why shouldn't I? I'm sure Noel and Francis would be very interested to know.'

'**No! Don't tell them! Oh, look, what do you want?**'

'I want you to join in with the nightmares.'

Geoff calmed down. He thought for a second, and seemed to decide that this might be a fair price for Hazel keeping his secret.

'**Well . . . all right. Deal. But I refuse to rehearse.**'

'What? You can't refuse to rehearse – how will you know what to do?'

Geoff grabbed her by the T-shirt again.

'**Just whisper to me on the night – all right? That's all you get! I'll be there at the nightmare, and you can tell me what to do, but I will** *not* **rehearse, and I will** *not* **take notes from you afterwards! Got it?**'

Hazel thought she better take the deal before Geoff got angrier.

'. . . OK.'

Geoff breathed slowly, twitched his whiskers, and whooshed out of the window and into the dawn. Hazel was left on the floor, feeling rather perplexed.

Isambard must miss his father, she thought. She didn't know *what* she would feel like if her father died. She began to feel very sad for him. She stood up, and quietly closed the door to his tower.

She hoped he liked his boot. He deserved a bit of happiness. Maybe, with that boot of his father's returned to him, and getting to see a performance of his play might cheer . . . *The play! She'd promised she'd perform the play tomorrow!*

The Tenth
Chapter of this Book

Isambard sat down at one end of Hazel's room, while she prepared her 'actors'. She'd managed less than three hours of rehearsing, and her performers certainly hadn't been doing any work on their parts in their spare time, as Eugenia made sure they didn't *have* any spare time. It was half two, and lunch had long ago been tidied away. The cast were all anxious to get back to their duties, but had agreed to at least finish the play.

Hazel felt queasy about the whole thing. The play – which wasn't very good, she had to admit – was Isambard's own way of protesting against his mother, and she had to make sure it encouraged him to be brave against her. But she's had *so* little time to rehearse, and she was *so* tired from all the nightmares.

For his part, Isambard looked happy. After his present from Geoff that morning, he seemed more relaxed than normal.

Hazel held her breath and counted to ten.

'OK, Isambard, we're ready to start.'

She gave Boynce the nod. He nodded back, and came out into the middle of the room, wearing a black bow tie just like Isambard wore.

'I am a mermaid! And . . .'

'No! Murderer!' whispered Hazel as loudly as she could.

Boynce looked confused. The play had only just begun. Pude and Dungeon were waiting nervously behind the bed with Hazel.

'I am a murderer! And I have a clever plan. My mother is a tyrant, and has always treated me badly! And I long to see her dead! Yes, audience, you will see a most terrible murmur tonight . . .'

'Murder! Murder!' whispered Hazel.

' . . . sorry, murder, a MURDER tonight. Watch out, Mother, pretty soon you'll be dead!'

Hazel looked at Mrs Dungeon. This was supposed to be her entrance. She was staring blankly at her knees. Hazel gave her a nudge.

'Oh, hello, dear, would you like some gravy?'

'No! It's your bit now! You have to go on the stage!' Hazel felt a bit silly saying this, as the 'stage' was only a different bit of her bedroom, but she didn't know how else to say it.

Mrs Dungeon walked out next to Boynce.

'I am Mary, and I am this boy's moth.'

'Mother! Mother!' But Mrs Dungeon didn't seem to hear her.

'I have tormented my lovely boy since he was just a Barbie — I have never washed him, or cooked for him, or sung him to sleep with sweet wallabies!'

'Lullabies! Lullabies!' Mrs Dungeon still didn't seem to hear her.

'I am a tyrant! But my pathetic son loves me anyway. You love me, don't you, son?'

Boynce looked a bit confused.

' . . . No! I hate you! I'm going to merger you!'

Isambard, despite mistakes, had started to giggle happily. Hazel shook her head frantically.

'No! You're supposed to lie to her! Don't let her know you're going to kill her! And it's MURDER!'

Boynce got the message.

'Yes, Mother! I love you, you are my favourite moth!'

But Mrs Dungeon didn't.

'Merger me! Whatever for? What are you going to merge me with?'

Isambard seemed to get excited at this bit, and started to shout out his own unhelpful comments.

'Merge her with a bat! No, wait, merge her with an octopus!'

He didn't seem to mind that they were messing up his play, but Hazel was fuming.

Boynce did his best to get the scene back on track.

'I didn't mean to say that, Mother. I would never mirror you. I am not a mirrorer! Come and sleep in this bed, and I will bring you some hot chocolate before bed!'

'Oh, you couldn't make it gravy, could you, dear? I like a nice bit of gravy.'

'That's not your line, Mrs Dungeon! You want hot chocolate!'

Mrs Dungeon didn't know *what* to do.

'But, dear, we don't HAVE any hot chocolate.'

Boynce seemed desperate. He did his best to help the play along.

'I am a marmoset! And I have a clever plan. I hate my mortar! And long to see her dead! Yes, audience, you will see a most terrible margarine tonight. Watch out, mortar, pretty soon you'll be dead!'

Hazel was furious.

'That's the beginning, Boynce! You've gone back to the beginning!'

Luckily, by this point Mrs Dungeon had got onto the bed and gone to sleep, just like she was supposed to. However, she wasn't acting being asleep, she'd just got tired and fancied a rest.

Boynce remembered where he was.

'Aha! The perfect opportunity! Now I will let a vicious tiger into her bedroom, and she will be horribly deaded!'

Amazingly, Mr Pude remembered his cue. He leapt onstage with a roar, and began crawling about on all fours. He was doing his best, but Hazel had to admit he still looked just like a potato.

'I'm a tiger! Raaaargh!!'

Isambard was laughing happily.

'Go! Go, tiger! Kill my mother! For I hate her, though I never told her!' screamed Boynce, passionately.

As Pude threw himself onto the bed, one of the legs broke, the whole thing collapsed, and Mrs Dungeon awoke with a start.

'What ARE you doing, Mr Pude! You're behaving like

an animal!'

'Raaargh!'

Isambard was really laughing now.

'No! Mrs Dungeon, you have to give the closing speech!'

'What dear?'

'The speech! The speech I wrote for you!'

Mrs Dungeon seemed to be remembering.

'I . . . I am so very sad to be dying . . . I don't know who could have put this tiger in my room . . . surely not my pathetic son, for he is a coward! Oh! What a horrible way to die! Mur . . . mar . . . mir . . . married? . . . yes! . . . married to a tiger!'

Mr Pude looked very pleased, took Mrs Dungeon's hand and kissed it. Boynce, trying to be helpful, started humming the wedding march.

Isambard stood up and applauded. The cast bowed, and Hazel threw her script to the ground.

'Sorry, dear, but we've got to be off now — work to be done. I hope you liked your play, Master Isambard,' said Boynce, tousling Isambard's hair.

'You two be down on time for dinner, all right? I've made a nice new vat of gravy for tonight.' Mrs Dungeon licked her lips and wandered off.

Mr Pude leaned next to Hazel's ear.

'Pity about all the words, eh? Still, he seems to have enjoyed it.'

When they were left alone, Isambard gave Hazel a big hug, as awkwardly as ever.

'Thank you! That was amazing! That was great!

Imagine her marrying her tiger! I'm sure she didn't hear us – you don't think she heard us do you? Thank you!'

He hugged her again.

'I'm sure if I ask them they can do it again some time. Hazel – this has been the best day ever!'

With that, he picked up the pages of the script from Hazel's floor, and skipped off to his room.

But Hazel didn't even wave goodbye. She had just had the idea for tonight's nightmare – tonight's nightmare that Geoff was going to be in, unless he wanted the others to know about his present. This was it – this was the night. Hazel just knew she was going to hear Eugenia scream.

* * *

From the diary of Lady Eugenia Pequierde:

I write this with trembling hands. It is early morning. I want to write down as much as I can of this last dream before I forget it.

It began with a rough, dry voice from the shadows. It spoke to me commandingly from beside my bed. It said something like –

'Hurry, miss – you'll be late for your performance! You don't want to be late for your performance, do you?'

I reached out to my bedside light in a daze, and turned it on to be confronted by the leopard–gorilla thing. It spoke to me just as a person might, and I was somewhere between shaking with fear and talking to him as I would talk to any human.

'Come on! Chop, chop! Chop, chop! CHOP! Get dressed – you don't want to keep your adoring audience waiting, miss!'

He wore a velvet smoking jacket, a starched white shirt, a smart bow tie, and a monocle. One of his vast, gorilla hands threw a dress on to my bed. It was covered in sequins, and glittered in the moonlight. I sat frozen, unable to speak or move.

'I must insist that you get dressed, miss – we need to do your make-up as well, and your adoring fans . . . '

I still could do nothing, and I felt myself begin to shake. He quickly became angry.

'FOR CRYING OUT LOUD JUST PUT THE STUPID DRESS ON.'

As quickly as I could, I threw the dress over my head. The monster turned his back on me until I had finished.

'Are you DONE yet?'

I am ashamed to say I begged pathetically – 'Please don't hurt me.' He looked at me with contempt.

'I'm not making any promises.'

Then he cocked his head, as if someone was whispering to him. It was very strange. He frowned in irritation, and then revised what he had first said.

'What I meant to say was that you look divine, miss – more beautiful than ever – your audience will be so happy.' He sighed again. 'Or something like that.'

He took my hand in his, and led me gently out of bed.

'This way! We must put your make-up on!'

I was confronted with the half-bird, half-frog thing. In its fat lips it held some red lipstick.

'Well? Hurry up! You must let your assistant put on your make-up. We don't have any time to spare.'

My heart sank – not for the first time that night. The frog-ostrich was clearly not going to come to me. I stepped towards it, and bent down.

The creature's face glistened with moisture. It smelt of old bath water. I held my breath as I lowered my face toward it.

Then, with a squelchy sound, the creature thrust the lipstick clumsily at my face, poking me in the nostril. It proceeded to draw a circle around the general area of my lips – far more slowly than I thought I could bear. When it was finished, it stepped away, and spat the lipstick onto the floor.

'THERE. ALL DONE. DON'T YOU LOOK NICE?'

By this point, I was mad with fright – though of course I did not cry.

'Now you are ready – ready for your delicious performance. I do look forward, with sumptuous anticipation to . . . to . . .' at this point, the monster seemed to talk to someone else – though I couldn't see who. It must have been the person he had listened to before. He spoke angrily, saying **'Do I HAVE to say all this rubbish!? I mean why don't I just throw her out of the window and be done with it? No I do NOT think it's scarier like this. What would be scary would be me tying you to a . . .** 'He sighed. **'Yes. Yes, all right.'** He turned back to me, and put his hand on the small of my back, and moved me to my window. There, below me, was an audience of beasts – the ducks from the lake, the dog, the pigs. **'Now, miss. You mustn't be nervous. They adore you. All they want to hear is your special song. If you just sing them your special song, they will be so very happy.'**

'My . . . my special song?' I replied.

'Yes! Don't you remember? It is SO moving. When I first heard it, I don't mind telling you I cried for three hours. The lyrics are the best thing. Do sing those wonderful lyrics again!'

Of course, I did not know the lyrics to this song. I was overwhelmed by the madness of my surroundings, and I screamed. It was, I am sure, the worst nightmare yet.

But in a moment the leopard-gorilla seemed to be angry again.

'What? What? Is this really the brilliant idea for the nightmare? Not remembering her lines? I've had scarier farts than this dream! This is nonsense!'

With that he fled out of my window. The ostrich-frog followed quickly, the audience dispersed, and I was alone. I was confused by him saying 'idea for the nightmare', as if these wretched figments of my imagination actually sat around planning my torments. Of course, I was glad the dream ended when it did . . .

* * *

'Do you think maybe that was just a little bit selfish of you, Geoff?'

Geoff didn't even look at Noel.

'The dream was no good. What does she care about forgetting her lines?'

Noel looked upset. The poor creature had spent the whole nightmare wedged into Geoff's smoking jacket, whispering his lines to him off the script Hazel had written. It had been Noel whom Geoff had been shouting at throughout.

'I THOUGHT SHE LOOKED PRETTY SCARED.'

But Hazel wasn't listening to the monsters bickering that night. She was thinking about Eugenia's scream.

When she had stepped out onto the balcony, it had finally happened – a scream. A scream of terror and helplessness from Lady Pequierde. Hazel smiled, and went off back to the house. She slept like a baby.

Hazel's mood was sunny that morning, and she woke up early at eleven, ready for the day.

The first thing she thought to do was go and have a nice chat with nice Mrs Dungeon. She'd forgotten all about the theatrical catastrophe of yesterday afternoon, and felt like a cosy natter over a jug of gravy might be the best way to spend the hour before lunch.

The kitchen smelt good.

That couldn't have been right. Could it?

Hazel peeped round the kitchen door to find Mrs Dungeon checking on a tray of parsnips roasting in the oven. After a week of being at a loss as to what to cook for a vegetarian, she'd finally stumbled across one of Hazel's favourites.

'Are you going to put maple syrup on those?'

Mrs Dungeon turned round from her tray and smiled.

'Oh yes, dear, they've plenty of maple syrup on them already — and do you know what else?'

135

Hazel prayed it wasn't gravy.

'What?'

Mrs Dungeon beckoned for her to come over to the steaming tray of neatly sliced parsnips. Hazel had a look at them. They smelled better than anything else that had been up Hazel's nose since she arrived.

'Wow!'

'Mmm, I know, lovely i'nt it? That's whole-grain mustard they've got on them – great big dollops of the stuff.'

Hazel couldn't wait to tuck in. She sat up on a high kitchen chair, and yawned.

'You're up early, dear. Sleep all right?'

'I slept great. Did you sleep well?'

'Oh yes, I slept very well. Although . . .' she dropped her voice to a whisper, 'I did come up with a little idea while I was nodding off.'

Saying no more, she went over to the sink, and opened the cupboard beneath it. Instantly, a cloud of smoke billowed out into the kitchen.

'Quack!'

Mrs Dungeon lifted a large metal basin out of the cupboard. In that basin sat a duck, puffing happily on a cigarette.

'Mrs Dungeon! Why are you keeping that poor duck under the sink?'

'He hasn't been there long dear – just long enough for the milk to absorb his flavour.'

As Mrs Dungeon put the basin onto the kitchen table, Hazel saw that the duck was floating in milk.

'See, if I can get the tea to smell of socks, I thought –

why not try to get the milk to smell of a duck? They're filthy creatures, an' I thought it'd make a real pong.'

Hazel held her nose over the milk to see if it was true. To be honest, the milk mostly smelled of cigarettes.

'I can't believe you're going to feed her this milk!'

Hazel stopped, and realised it was a bit rich being surprised at Mrs Dungeon when the night before she herself had dressed a gorilleopard up in a velvet jacket and sent it into Eugenia's room to frighten her senseless.

'Well, my dearie, the important thing is to strain the milk so there aren't any duck feathers left in it – her ladyship'd get pretty suspicious if she found a feather in her tea!'

They both laughed delightedly. Hazel decided it was a very good idea indeed. Dungeon patted the duck on the head, and it quacked merrily.

'I think Master Isambard enjoyed the play yesterday, didn't he?'

Hazel suddenly remembered the whole mess.

'Oh! Yeah . . . sure. He seemed pleased. He's a bit weird sometimes.'

Dungeon put a hand on Hazel's shoulder.

'He's a sad little boy, dear. Never got over the death of his old dad, bless him. Terrible thing to happen to a lad.'

She shook her head and began to get plates out for lunch.

Hazel had forgotten that there used to be someone else living in this house. Someone they'd all known, who'd been very important to them.

'DUNGEON!'

Eugenia's voice echoed down the hall from her drawing

room. Mrs Dungeon jumped, dropping one of the plates she'd been holding. She muttered to herself while sweeping it up as quickly as she could. It must be horrible hearing that voice screeching at you all day, thought Hazel.

'Oh my! She's already finished the last mug I gave her!'

She turned the kettle on and threw a teabag in a mug. Like lightning, she grabbed a bowl of sugar out of the cupboard, dropped in two spoonfuls, turned the kettle off just before it boiled and poured it in, sloshing hot water onto her hands.

'Ow! Ow!'

She shooed the duck out of the basin, poured a generous helping of milk out of the basin into the mug, and disappeared out of the door in a flash.

'Quack!'

Hazel shuddered at the thought of following Eugenia's orders all day, never getting so much as a please or thank you . . .

Wait! The milk! She hadn't drained the milk— in her rush she'd just poured it straight in — there might be feathers in it!

Hazel raced towards the drawing room, skidding on the stone floor. Dungeon was just closing the door.

'Wait!' yelled Hazel, as she charged in after her.

Eugenia was sat in her ugly brown chair, legs curled up beneath her, a magazine in her hands. She was holding the mug! Dungeon was plumping one of the mouldy old cushions behind her.

Without looking up, Eugenia sneered, 'What on earth are you yelling about, you stupid girl?'

Hazel thought about that arrogant expression changed

to a scream, as it had been last night, when Eugenia wasn't so tough.

'I . . . I was helping with lunch and . . . just wanted to ask if Mrs Dungeon wanted me to, um, drain the milk?'

Hazel winked, and Mrs Dungeon's face fell. She looked terrified.

'My dear girl, as if it isn't bad enough you lowering yourself to the level of a servant by preparing a meal, you seem to have utterly misunderstood the whole process of cooking. There is absolutely no culinary practice, known to man or beast, that goes by the name of "draining the milk".'

Hazel giggled.

'Oh yeah! Stupid me . . . I meant — do you want me to take the parsnips out of the oven?'

Dungeon nodded stiffly, still dumbstruck with fear. Hazel left the room, and pressed her eye against the crack in the door. She hoped Mrs Dungeon could think of something before Eugenia tried to drink the tea.

But from the expression on her face, it didn't look like she was in any state to be coming up with a clever plan. She stood uselessly behind the chair.

'Dungeon, could you please get those mushrooms off the sofa.'

Dungeon gulped. Eugenia must be in a very bad mood to notice the mushrooms — normally they didn't bother her at all. Still keeping one eye on the mug she pulled a dish cloth out of her apron, and began to pick the mushrooms off the yellow material. As she wasn't looking what she was doing, she mostly just smeared the mushrooms into the sofa. All of a sudden she had a plan.

'Oh, ma'am — you must let me give that chair a quick wipe . . . if you just hand me the magazine and the tea you can sit on the sofa . . .'

'You will do nothing of the sort — do stop drivelling, woman. Would you give this table a dust while you're at it.'

Dungeon jumped up from the sofa as quickly as she could, produced a duster from the folds of her dress, and poked frantically at the table. Using wild, swirling movements, she was presumably hoping to knock the mug out of Eugenia's hand. Instead all she managed to do was tickle her nose.

'Ack! Ack! Get away from me! What on earth is wrong with you? Get away from the table — you can dust it when I've gone to bed.'

This of course meant doing it in the middle of the night. Dungeon's day was going from bad to worse.

'Now before you go, clean my boots.' Eugenia stuck one leg unceremoniously onto her footstool.

Dungeon hunkered down onto the floor with some difficulty, and spat on the boots.

'What are you doing?!'

'Well, sorry, ma'am, but we don't have any money for boot polish, so it's just going to have to be a cloth and some spit.'

Eugenia groaned, and waved for her to continue. Mind racing, Dungeon absent-mindedly scrubbed at the boots, before suddenly making her next move.

With some effort she heaved Eugenia's boot up — as if she was trying to clean the heel — but with the actual intention of causing her to spill her tea. The effect, rather than the intention, was to knock the whole chair backwards on to the floor, carrying Eugenia with it.

'Aaaargh! How . . . why . . . what are you doing, you oaf?!'

Eugenia flailed clumsily like a beetle on its back. Dungeon, despite her advanced years, made a good go of lifting the chair back up into place, grunting as she did.

As she set the chair back down on the damp carpet, she realised to her horror that Eugenia was still holding the mug of tea. She'd managed to keep it from spilling!

'I am so sorry, ma'am – I was just trying to clean your heel, and I suppose I went a bit far.'

'One of these days, Dungeon, I am going to cave your skull in with a shovel and bury you in the garden! Never, *ever*, do that again!'

She sighed with the weight of years of this sort of abuse.

'Yes, ma'am.'

The tea was still there.

She wrung her hands, and muttered quiet nothings to herself, shifting from foot to foot. Hazel, still listening from outside the door, bit her hand to stop from screaming, and prayed for a miracle.

'Ma'am – are you *sure* you want that tea?'

Eugenia looked at her as if she had just said the earth was flat.

'What could possibly have put that thought in your head?'

Having been reminded of her tea, Eugenia lifted it towards her lips and blew on it to cool it down as she always did.

'No! I . . . I forgot to put milk in it!'

Eugenia stopped.

'Dear God, you're revolting. How can you possibly have failed to put milk in a cup of tea? Sometimes I think your mother dropped a bag full of hammers on your head as a baby.'

With no further ado, she passed the mug to Dungeon, who took it gratefully, and turned to get out as quickly as possible.

'Wait!'

Oh dear.

'Now you mention it, maybe I shouldn't always have milk in my tea. I suppose it's fattening, isn't it? Yes, you'd know all about fattening. If you have milk in your tea, maybe I should have mine without. Give me that mug.'

Dungeon nearly whimpered.

'*Give* it to me, you imbecile.'

She returned the mug to her, and stood paralysed by the chair.

'Thank you. Now . . . wait a minute, this has plenty of milk in it.'

She gazed into her tea.

'What on earth are you talking about? This obviously has milk . . . eeek!'

Eugenia put the mug down, and wiped her hands disgustedly on the chair.

Hazel thought, afterwards, that the whole business that followed was in a way her fault. If she hadn't done such a good nightmare beforehand, Eugenia wouldn't have been in such an incredibly foul mood, and would perhaps have been just a tiny bit more merciful. But there was *no* excuse for what Eugenia did next. Besides, the nightmare and the feathers were only things she deserved.

Eugenia was perfectly still now, like a snake about to strike. She thought for a moment before speaking, and when she opened her mouth, her voice was quiet and menacing.

'Mrs Dungeon?'

'Yes ma'am?'

'Are there feathers in my tea?'

' . . . Yes, ma'am.'

'Right. Mrs Dungeon – did you put . . . a *duck* in my tea?'

' . . . Yes, ma'am.'

Now Eugenia stood up. She so rarely stood up.

'I want you to go and fetch Boynce, and I want you to go and fetch Pude. You are to inform them that they, like you, are now unemployed. The three of you do not work here any more, and you shall never work anywhere where I have influence.'

Dungeon spluttered.

'But, ma'am, you can't be serious! They haven't done nothin' – it was all me . . .'

'I expect *all* of your disgusting possessions to be removed from the house by the end of the day. I expect every single crumb of food to remain in the kitchen. I expect your rooms to be scrubbed and cleaned. And if I ever see you on my land again, I will, quite simply, shoot you.'

Dungeon could barely speak.

'But . . . but . . .'

Eugenia sat back down in her chair, and looked to her magazine. Hazel thought that it took a special, terrible sort of anger to sit there so calmly while Mrs Dungeon's life fell apart.

'I'm not interested in what you have to say. Get out of my sight this instant.'

She began to read her magazine, as if she was the only person in the room.

Dungeon, now silent, turned and walked out of the room, closing the door as she went.

Hazel didn't know what to say. She'd never had a job, and her dad had never lost his. Where were they all going to go? Where would they get money? How long had they worked here? Would she ever see them again?

In the end, she said nothing, and simply sat on the stairs and listened as Dungeon, Pude and Boynce, with hardly any fuss at all, tidied up their things and cleaned their rooms.

This was it. This was the final straw. Eugenia couldn't treat people like this any more – she *had* to be taught a lesson.

Though she had not yet been able to put it into words, a plan had been formulating in her mind for a while. She thought back to Geoff with that boot; to Isambard's happiness the morning after he received it; to what Dungeon had said that morning about Isambard never getting over his father's death; to her memories of tall, dashing Podbury Pequierde.

If she really wanted to scare Eugenia, what should she make a dream about? Hazel thought she knew what. Now was the time. Tonight was the night. Revenge would be Hazel's, at last.

As she was leaving the house, Mrs Dungeon lent down to give Hazel a big hug, and a kiss on the cheek. Whilst holding her, she whispered in her ear.

'I've left a nice pot of gravy in the fridge for you, dear. You take care of yourself.'

Then, with a wink, at about nine o'clock at night, she left for good.

The Twelfth Chapter of this Book

Lady Eugenia Pequierde never wrote a word in her diary about her next nightmare.

Night fell again on that dilapidated house. Owls began to hoot in the woods, and the spiders crawled out on to their webs in Isambard's attic. The ducks were quiet on their lake. The pigs sat awake in their pen. Bullivant stood guard outside his kennel, watching out for danger, though he was unable to see or hear a thing.

Eugenia had finished eating her dinner, and drinking her tea, and brushing her teeth, and getting into her nightie. She was anxious: about living without servants for the first time in years; about still having that stupid girl in her house; but most of all about her dream from last night. She wished she didn't have to have a nightmare again. She didn't know what she was in for.

She savoured the last, precious drop of tea before braving her bed. She set the mug on her bedside table as she did every night.

The table had been lovely once. But the mahogany had chipped, circular tea-stains disfigured the top, and dust covered every inch of it. Just to underline how terribly unpleasant Eugenia's bedside table was, let me remind you that dust is dead skin. Layer after layer of dead skin, falling like snow on to the furniture of your house. So the next time you feel like eating food that's fallen on the carpet, or licking the television, just remember that you might as well be chewing off your own arm.

On Eugenia's table was a snowdrift of human skin quite sufficient to make a new Eugenia out of. On to this dreadful table she set her mug. It was one of hundreds, each one brown and featureless.

She turned out the light, hauled the pungent sheets over her shoulders, and cursed the night – it was somehow always cold in her room, though it was high summer. Then she waited, tense, knowing what was coming.

Sure enough, she began to hear footsteps. Eager to get on with the nightmare, she rushed to turn on the light.

Without any scratching, or whispering, or waiting, or anticipation of any kind, the nightmare began. The half-gorilla, half-leopard thing was standing in her room. It was wearing an ill-fitting black jacket, a wig of thick, curly, black hair, and a fake moustache.

'**Eugenia, my darling. I'm back. It's me – Podbury.**'

She let out a gasp. Then she started to cry.

Eugenia, sitting there in her nightie, eyes filled with tears, looked suddenly like a little girl. It was if years had suddenly been taken away from her – the last few years of bitterness and anger floated from her and out the window, and she was left as she had been when Podbury was alive — younger, more vulnerable, full of hope.

Geoff walked to the bed, and put his vast arm around Eugenia's shoulders — just as Podbury had once done. He looked at her, though she could not look at him.

Then, slowly, she reached out a hand to him. It shook very slightly in the lamplight, as it touched the curls of thick, black hair. She ran her fingers through that hair, still unable to look her dead husband in the eye.

'**Will you come gambling with me, darling? Just one more roll of the dice, eh? I've missed you.**' The creature took her hand in his, and held it tightly.

Eugenia continued to cry quietly, but stood up.

The creature walked her over to the window, where a roulette wheel was sitting on a table. Eugenia could not see where it might have come from, but she didn't care. It was very quiet in the room. No other monsters — just this one. No moaning, or shaking, or singing. She couldn't hear the owls or wood-pigeons outside. Everyone else in the house was surely asleep. There was no moon. It was the dead of night, and Eugenia was all alone, with no monsters but this one.

She put one shaking hand on the lapel of his jacket, and said, in a thin voice, 'Oh, Podbury! I've missed you so much. I've been so lonely without you.' The effort of speaking was enormous — and her voice was small and high like a child.

The creature picked up the silver ball of the roulette wheel.

'Come now, my sweet. Don't cry. I want you to place one last bet with me. What shall it be?'

Eugenia was limp in Geoff's arms, like a doll. She looked at the numbered red and black pockets of the wheel. His arms were strong as they supported her, just like when he was alive. She wanted only to hug him, but, with the strange urgency of dreams, knew that she had to choose quickly. She and Podbury always bet on the same number.

'Black eight, my darling. Always black eight at the roulette table,' she said.

He nodded. Podbury always bet with confidence and flair. A little nod of the head, a shot of whisky, and away he went. He spun the wheel, and the red and black pockets blurred as they rotated. He threw the silver ball in, and it clattered around noisily.

As they waited for the ball to land, Eugenia lent up to the leopard-ear of the creature, which was furry and warm, and whispered into it.

'Please stay.'

Hazel, who was watching from her tree, felt her stomach turn. She had never seen Eugenia like this. She had never seen anyone like this.

The silver ball landed, and the wheel spun slowly to a stop.

Red thirty-four.

The creature looked at her with its big, dark eyes. It was very tall, and Eugenia craned her neck to look at it.

'I'm so sorry, my darling. We lost the bet. Red thirty-four. I'm so sorry.'

Eugenia laughed. Just like old times. Podbury always lost the bet – her dark, unlucky prince.

'No! Its fine! I don't mind. I don't care about the money – I just want you to stay.'

The creature held her gaze.

'No. You don't understand. We lost the bet. I have to leave. If you'd picked red thirty-four I could have stayed, but I have to leave.'

Eugenia tried not to cry.

'But . . . why . . . I don't understand?!'

Podbury began to let go of her, and she held onto him more tightly. He let out a low, rumbling sigh, and looked her straight in the eye again.

'I made a deal.'

She held on even tighter.

'What do you mean? What deal? What do you mean you made a deal?'

He moved his face very close to hers. She could smell his leopard breath.

'A deal with the devil. The deal was that if we could win just one round of roulette, he'd let me stay. But we lost.'

Her knees felt weak. She gasped for breath.

'No! No! You're in hell!?'

He stroked her hair.

'Yes.'

Eugenia screamed. Not like last night. Not because something weird, and gruesome, and foul confronted her. But because she felt she was being torn apart. Because she didn't know if she could bear to lose Podbury again.

Because the worst thing that ever happened to her was happening again. Even if it was only a dream. The creature held her very tightly, and she buried her head in its fur. She heard its heart beating.

'Goodbye,' it whispered, as it let go of her. It turned away, and climbed out of the window.

Eugenia fell to the floor, helpless. She didn't get any sleep that night. She just cried. She cried huge, shuddering sobs. She cried until her tears ran dry – cried until morning, cried all night, on that same spot in the middle of the floor.

* * *

Hazel felt terrible.

'I feel terrible,' she said, truthfully.

She'd never felt guilt like this before. It was like Eugenia had crawled, sobbing and whimpering, into the inside of Hazel's eyelids, and would not go away.

The dream had certainly been a success – if that wasn't Eugenia feeling sorry, Hazel didn't know what was. Just as she had done when Geoff brought Isambard the boot, she thought about how she would feel if her dad died. Then she thought what it would be like if someone dressed up as her dad, came into her room at night, and said . . . the things that Geoff had said to Eugenia.

Hazel felt very small, and very heavy – like a marble. She didn't want to talk. She didn't want to go to bed. She didn't know how she was ever going to stand up from the log she was sitting on, and what she was going to do after she did.

'Can I have a biscuit, Francis?'

Francis was very quiet, as was Noel. They hadn't said anything since the nightmare finished. Noel just sat there, next to his mirror, not looking into it. Francis fetched his biscuits from under some bushes, and brought them over to Hazel.

'ARE YOU OK?'

'No.'

Hazel stared straight ahead. At least she had her friends. Francis was so nice to jump right up and give her a biscuit – she was sure with their help she'd feel better soon. She even reached out and gave Francis a friendly pat on the leg.

'WE THOUGHT YOU'D BE HAPPY.'

Hazel looked up at him, very surprised.

'What do you mean? Didn't you see her?'

Francis shuffled from one foot to the other.

'BUT I THOUGHT THAT'S WHAT WE WERE TRYING TO DO?'

Hazel's mouth fell open. She looked to Noel, who nodded in agreement.

'*Wasn't this what you wanted?*'

Hazel was *sure* this wasn't what she'd wanted – she'd never meant to hurt Eugenia like that. What must Francis and Noel think of her?

'No! That's not what I wanted! I just wanted to scare her a bit – but tonight I felt really bad! No one deserves to feel like that.'

Noel and Francis said nothing, but stared at her blankly. She was very puzzled that they weren't rushing to agree with her.

'I think . . . I think what we did tonight was wrong. I think we should stop the nightmares!'

This was clearly a surprise. Her two friends looked to each other in panic, as if they wanted to speak but could not.

'What's wrong with you? We can't possibly make the poor woman any more miserable than we've already made her!'

'BUT WE'RE NIGHTMARES! THAT'S WHAT WE'RE SUPPOSED TO DO.'

'Yeah, and you've taught us to be so much better! That's the best nightmare we've ever done. We can't give up now.'

Hazel couldn't believe she was hearing this.

'How can you say that! She was crying!'

There was silence at the camp. They all looked at each other, all baffled. The owls could be heard in the distance. The fire had burned down to its embers. Nobody knew what to say.

Except Geoff.

He unfurled from his place by the fire, and padded on all fours towards Hazel, his tail dancing in the orange light. He sat on his haunches directly in front of her. His breath was hot on her face.

He had a very strange look in his eyes. Hazel felt a deep sense of fear that she could not explain, bubbling up from her stomach, tightening her throat and drying her mouth. She had a sense that something terrible was about to happen.

'We will not stop. It is not yet time to stop. We . . . are . . . not . . . finished.'

Every one of those last four words was said as if spitting into Hazel's face. She had no idea what he meant, but she felt absolute dread at his words.

'Noel! Francis! What's Geoff talking about? Get him away from me!'

But they did nothing. Though they were supposed to be her friends, they just stood there. Geoff grinned a toothy, smelly, leopard's grin.

'**We are not finished. We won't be finished . . . until . . . she's . . . dead.**'

Hazel held very tightly onto the log, and refused to believe what Geoff was saying.

'Geoff, stop saying that – you're scaring me!'

Why weren't the others doing anything? They simply stared at her, looking helpless.

'**What do you think we were doing all this time, little girl?**'

'What do you mean? We were trying to scare her – but now we've gone too far!'

'**We have not gone nearly far enough. We have not simply been trying to scare her. We have been trying to scare her to death.**'

Hazel was laughing nervously. It had all started to seem ridiculous. Of course they weren't trying to kill her – she'd spent the last week and a half with these creatures, and she knew for certain that they weren't killers.

'Geoff, don't be silly – you're nightmares, not murderers!'

'**No. We're both.**'

Noel had a ghostly expression on his face.

'THAT'S WHAT ISAMBARD WHATS US TO DO. TO KILL HER.'

Hazel's heart skipped a beat.

She looked around at the monsters in front of her, and it occurred to her that that's exactly what they were – monsters. She turned from Francis's glistening, warty face, thick with slime, a meaty tongue darting out from between his green lips; to Noel's sharp little nose sniffing the air, venomous fangs visible from beneath his lips, two beady, dark eyes staring back at her; to Geoff's terrible jaws, slightly open as he breathed, teeth as big as eggs jutting out from his black lips. They *were* monsters.

'What does Isambard have to do with this?'

Geoff laughed. The hot air from his mouth blew Hazel's hair back like a thunderstorm.

'**He made us.**'

' . . . What?'

'**He *made* us. Didn't you know? He's very clever, you see? Very clever *indeed*. And that terrible woman has put him through hell. He made us to be his revenge.**'

He laughed again.

'**Where did you think we came from? Do you think we simply appeared out of thin air? He *built* us. We are his creations.**'

Francis and Noel said nothing. They were not going to contradict him.

'I don't believe you!'

'**It doesn't matter whether you believe us. I know you and Francis and Noel have been having a lot of fun pratting around for a week – but this is serious work we are doing. Eugenia . . . must . . . die.**'

'But you're not like that! You aren't murderers! You're my

friends . . .'

'We *are* like that.'

Noel nodded. Francis nodded. Geoff smiled. It dawned on her just how dangerous they were. A bite from Noel; a kick from Francis; a claw from Geoff — and she would be dead in a moment.

Hazel, shaking, fled. She didn't know what else to do. She didn't look back to see what they were doing. These weren't her friends — they were a gang of monsters, and nothing else. She found herself beginning to cry as she sprinted over bushes and roots, charging frantically through the trees, scratching her face as she had done when she first ran into that place. She prayed the monsters were not chasing after her — she prayed they would not eat her!

Now, as well as Eugenia crying helpless on the floor, the faces of those monsters were on the inside of her eyelids. She could not stop seeing Geoff's smile, and the others staring blankly, hopelessly back at her. These were not the faces of friends. She had no friends. She had lost her friends. She didn't want them to be her friends.

So off she ran, friendless, into that dark, uncertain forest.

around it. Hazel felt very sad thinking about what had happened to lovely Mrs Dungeon. She opened the fridge, and grabbed a slice of bread. She gobbled it as she scurried past the empty bedrooms on the ground floor.

She went past Eugenia's drawing room on her way to the stairs. It was strange to think of her now. Instead of imagining her waiting on her brown chair, ready to leap out and torture innocent passers-by, Hazel could only think of her on the floor, crying pathetically. It occurred to her that there must be photographs of Podbury in the drawing room – in fact the framed picture she saw Eugenia gazing at on that first night must have been of him!

As she went up past her bedroom she dropped off her rucksack, and tried to stop panicking. She needed to be calm and strong. 'No, Isambard – don't kill your mother. It's wrong. Bad Isambard!' She grimaced. She would have to think of something better than 'Bad Isambard'.

The attic was in dawn light now, and the cobwebs there lit up like Christmas decorations. The dust swirling through the air was clearly visible, and just looking at it made Hazel want to cough.

She half expected the door to be locked, but it opened smoothly onto the steep, grimy, spiral staircase that led to the tower. Hazel took a deep breath. The staircase curved round several times before ending at a trapdoor. Though this trapdoor was made of ancient, rotten wood, it was used regularly, and opened smoothly on well-oiled hinges.

As she emerged out of the trapdoor, she got her first look at Isambard's room.

The room was bigger than she'd expected. It was all

stone, and where other rooms in the house seemed to belong in a house, this one belonged in a castle. The windows were very narrow, and the ceiling was made of huge wooden beams. The walls and floor were bare stone. At night it was lit by an iron chandelier that looked more like a weapon than a decoration.

There were three tables — big oak ones, with lots of cupboard space beneath. There were lots of objects with sheets over them — old furniture, it looked like. There was also what looked like an old jail, with rusted iron bars. She couldn't see a bed anywhere. Wasn't this his bedroom? Maybe he slept somewhere else, which made this . . . his laboratory! Was this where he had made his monsters?

It must have been, and the proof was on the tables. Test tubes. Knives. Saws. Drills. Antiseptic. Bandages. Bloodstains. Chains for holding down things that did not want to be held down. Electrodes. Syringes. Bunsen burners.

'Hello!'

Isambard was already awake, and had been standing the other side of the trap door. He was fully dressed, in his black suit and bow tie.

'What are you doing here?'

Hazel blurted out the first thing that came into her head.

'Bad Isambard!'

He looked mortified.

'What? What did I do?'

He'd been holding a huge leather-bound book, which he now set down on a table.

Hazel tried to talk intelligently.

'I know everything! I've met your monsters!'

'I know! Isn't it *wonderful!*'

Hazel was surprised. He already knew! In a way, it was only logical that he knew what his monsters were up to — being their creator.

'Seriously, Hazel, thank you so much for everything you've done!'

Hazel's stomach sank.

'Everything I've done?'

He skipped over and gave her a hug. She could see all around the Pequierde estate from the tower — including the monsters' camp. It wasn't anywhere near as far away as it had seemed in the dark, and Isambard must have been able to watch her every night.

'Look, Isambard — how did you make them? I don't understand!'

He blushed, very proud.

'Well — I *am* very clever!' he giggled happily, 'And besides, I've so much time on my hands — there's nothing else to do but tinker around in my lab.'

'Where . . . where did you find the . . . parts . . . to make them out of?'

'Oh, I ordered them. They're mostly from reserves in Africa — Dad had black-market contacts out in Tanzania and Kenya from his safari days.'

Podbury's study! The address book was full of poachers! Isambard had been going in there to order animals! It was amazing to think of the effort involved in getting an ostrich or a gorilla shipped over from Tanzania. Isambard was very clever. Hazel was almost impressed.

'Do you know the poachers even offered to send me an elephant! It's all been pretty difficult – especially when the leopard I used to make Geoff bit Bullivant's head off! Poor old Bullivant! He didn't know *what* was happening – and then the leopard bit Jerry's leg off, or maybe Jilly's – and of course the ducks had endless fights with all the animals turning up. That's how they got so stressed, you know.'

Hazel's head was spinning.

'And you . . . cut them up . . . and . . . and . . .'

'Put them back together again in new ways! It worked better than I ever could have hoped. Dad loved leopards, and he loved gorillas, and I combined them into one extra-special creature – Geoff! Of course the leopard and the gorilla didn't want to be cut into pieces, but he's a whole new creature now, with a personality all of his own! The same goes for Francis and Noel!'

The monsters that Hazel used to think of as her friends had been made here – in this place of torture and misery. Animals had been kidnapped from their homes in Africa, cut up into bits, and made into . . . Noel, Francis and Geoff.

'Anyway, Hazel, I really want to say thank you for everything you've done for me. The play was great – but your nightmares have been amazing! I mean, not all of them worked, but . . .'

'No! No, that's what I wanted to talk to you about – I didn't mean to hurt your mum so much . . .'

Isambard didn't seem to want to listen to her.

'Nonsense! You're a genius! That one with the cushions

was a bit weird, but other than that, you've done miles better than I was doing! I was getting nowhere!'

Isambard seemed so happy he was almost jumping up and down.

He pulled a stool from beside a desk for her to sit on, and perched himself on a table.

Hazel stayed standing.

'I mean, I knew how to make them – but I didn't know what to do with them. That's where you came in! I had no idea you'd turn out to be so good at scaring people. My mother's been terrified!'

He was giggling excitedly, and as he became happier, Hazel became more horrified.

'But, Isambard, they said you're trying to scare her to death!'

'Of course I am! Of course I am! But I haven't known how! Those monsters have been trying their best – but last night! Last night you finally showed us how to do it! You gave us the secret, and now . . .' he gave Hazel a friendly little wink . . . 'I think I've come up with a nightmare of my own that'll finally finish her off!'

Hazel was flabbergasted. Isambard was completely insane. Certainly he was clever, but all those brains were clearly very dangerous. Hazel couldn't believe how much she'd underestimated him. She clenched and unclenched her fists, and tried to stay calm. This wasn't going to be the easy talk she'd hoped for.

She knew she had to be very careful. If he really was trying to kill his mother, she was going to have to use just the right words to persuade him not to.

'Well, about that, I was going to ask if maybe you should . . . NOT do it?'

Isambard looked totally gob-smacked. He had obviously thought Hazel was on his side. But then, a look Hazel had not seen before crept into his eyes – the steely look of a killer.

'Oh, sorry – I definitely have to kill her. Anything else I can help you with?'

He'd completely ignored her! How could he be talking so coldly about killing his own mother!

'What? No – just the mother thing. I mean, why do you want to do it?'

He didn't even have to think.

'She's a bad person. She brings nothing good to the world. She takes nothing good out of it. She only makes people unhappy.'

'Well I'm sure that can't be true . . .'

'She's *my* mother, not yours.'

He stared her down, not blinking, utterly sure of himself. She'd *definitely* never seen him like this. It was all a lot less subtle than Hazel had expected. She thought that he should be at least a *little* more ashamed of planning a murder.

'Well, what if everyone did what you're planning to do?'

'What do you mean?'

'What if Mrs Dungeon decided *she* wanted to kill *you*?'

'Oh, Mrs Dungeon definitely wouldn't want to kill me. I'm sure of it.'

'That's not the point. Let's say I wanted to kill you . . .'

'You don't want to kill me, do you?'

'Well, no, but I might.'

'You *might*! You're taking this far too lightly, Hazel! You can't just kill someone without knowing for certain it's the right thing to do.'

'Yes, I know, but . . . no, hang on . . . what if someone wanted to kill you to steal all your pets?'

'Oh. That would be awful.' Isambard appeared very concerned. Then he had an idea. 'I'd kill them first!'

' . . . But what if everyone just killed whoever they wanted? There'd be no one left.'

'Oh! That's a good point. You're right, we can't just go around killing whoever we want. We should only kill people who *deserve* to die.'

'But how do you know who deserves to die?' Hazel felt very clever for making this point. 'If the government is going to . . .'

'The decision should only be made by clever people like me who are never wrong.'

Hazel didn't know what to think. He was still the same Isambard — ten years old, pale, frightened. How was he saying things like this?

'Doesn't killing people do something bad to you? It makes you a murderer.'

'It's good for you! Stretches your body *and* your mind. Nine out of ten athletes recommend it.'

Isambard giggled crazily.

'That is NOT true.'

'Maybe not, but history's great heroes have been murderers! Napoleon! Julius Caesar! Genghis Khan!'

'I don't think they were goodies, Isambard. If you kill a bad person, I think that makes you bad too. Maybe as bad as them. Look, please, I just want you to tell me why! Why do you want to kill your mother?'

Suddenly Isambard became very angry. Somehow the last thing she had said really upset him. He puffed out his cheeks and glared at her. This was a whole new side to him, and for the first time in his company, Hazel was genuinely scared of him.

He stood up, walked towards the door, then back again, began to speak, then stopped. He was very upset.

'I don't want to talk to you! Just . . . just . . .' He had an idea.

He opened one of the cupboards in the desk, and pulled something out. He put it on the table. It was a severed human hand, stood on a little platform as if it were a stuffed bird. Hazel felt a bit sick.

Isambard pointed to it.

'There. Talk to the hand.'

He looked very pleased with himself.

'Isambard! That isn't what that means! When people say that, they hold up their *own* hand! You got this off American TV, didn't you?'

'Yes, and I know exactly what I'm doing. I no longer want to talk to you, so you must talk to this. My Talking Hand.'

She realised the thing had a little label saying 'Talking Hand'.

Hazel was very frustrated now.

'When Americans do it, they hold up their hand and say "Talk to the hand, cos the face ain't listenin'." You don't need a separate hand to do it.'

'It is much better this way, you stupid girl! Now I can tell you to talk to the hand, and simply leave the room.'

And with that he stormed off down his trapdoor.

Hazel looked at the hand. She stood up and stared closely at it.

'Hello?'

The hand did not respond.

What was she going to do? Where had he gone? What if he was off to kill his mother right now!

But Isambard came back in a moment later, still angry. Geoff was with him. He'd followed her back, and she hadn't heard a thing!

'I'm fed up of talking to you now! Geoff, make her go to sleep!'

Hazel yelped as Geoff, who used to sort of be her friend, thwacked her on the head with his massive gorilla hand. As she passed out, she thought she saw him smiling.

The Fourteenth Chapter of this Book

I am happy. It is summer.

My name is Eugenia. Eugenia Pequierde. Eugenia, Lady Pequierde. My husband is a rich and powerful man. He is handsome, and tall, and brave, and strong. His name is Sir Podburdy Bewley Pequierde.

I am beautiful. I am a Lady. I am a mother.

My beautiful baby boy is called Isambard Pequierde. He has dark hair and eyes like his father, but he has my pale skin.

I am walking with Isambard holding my hand. His hand is warm and soft, like a little mouse. He is five years old, and the smartest boy in his class.

I have been a mother for five years, and a wife for twelve.

I am walking in the sunshine with Isambard holding my hand, and I am beautiful, and my husband's name is Sir Podbury Bewley Pequierde.

I am happy.

We are walking in London Zoo, on the hottest day of the year. The sky is blue, and vast. The trees are green, and flourishing. The sun is yellow and kind.

Isambard wants to see the tigers.

He says 'Please, Mother, may I see the tigers with their jaws?'

I say, 'Yes — because you are good boy, you may see whatever you like.'

Podbury turns and smiles at us. He is walking ahead, swinging a silver-topped cane. He wears a pair of shorts and sandals, and grins as the sun warms his face.

Isambard squeezes my hand, and pulls it to him, and kisses it like a gentleman. He asks for so little.

He is carrying a chocolate ice-cream, and it is dripping on his shirt and socks. I do not mind.

I am wearing a blue dress and sandals. My feet are warm — as warm as if I was sitting in front of a fire. My blonde hair blows about my face in the breeze. Podbury turns again to look at us. Then he stops, and waits for us to catch up with him.

As I walk towards him, he puts his arm around me and kisses my cheek. Then he picks Isambard up in his arms, and points to an enclosure where a walrus is sunning itself on a beach. The walrus yawns, showing its teeth. Isambard gasps, and laughs in wonder. He has never seen a walrus before. Podbury has shown him his first walrus.

We stand there, in the sun, and I am happy.

'A tiger!' pipes Isambard, and Podbury laughs.

'That's not a tiger, little man. How do we know it's not a tiger?'

Isambard only has to think for a second.

'Because it has no stripes!'

'Exactly, Lieutenant Isambard, good knowledge! Now, if you march this way, I and Colonel Mum will show you where the tigers are!'

'Yes, General Dad!'

We all salute, and walk again, in the zoo, in London, in the sun. I hug Podbury tightly, and run a hand through his black hair.

'Oh no!' yelps Isambard.

He has dropped his ice-cream.

It is melting quickly into a puddle of chocolate on the ground. The cone sticks up like a tower. A fly begins to buzz around it.

'Not to worry, Lieutenant Isambard, I shall return to the supply base, and fetch you another ice-cream. Would you like that?'

'Thank you!'

Isambard hugs his father, and I continue to walk to the tigers while Podbury runs to the ice-cream stand. He turns to me and waves.

I ruffle Isambard's soft hair. I smile. I point to where a gorilla sits in the shade, under a tree. The gorilla is very still, and seems almost to be waiting for something. His hands are so strange — almost like a man's.

We keep walking, past the porcupine's enclosure. It has had its breakfast, and lies, full, by a stream. Its spines bristle.

I decide to walk through the dark of the reptile house, and we stop to look at a python, and a colourful frog.

As we leave, returning to the bright sunshine, we see an

ostrich stretching its wings.

Beyond it, I see the leopard's cage, but the leopard is hiding today.

I wonder what the gorilla was waiting for?

Finally, we arrive at the tigers.

They are so beautiful — like something from a dream. Their fur is deep orange, and white, and black. Their fur is shiny, and moves like an ocean when they walk. They are walking up and down, prowling back and forth. They have not been fed.

'Tigers!'

'Yes, Isambard, tigers!'

The tigers' enclosure is sunk into the ground, and Isambard runs to the railing, and looks down into it with awe. The tigers look back up at him, with yellow, flashing eyes. Their enclosure is lush and green, with a lake, and a forest.

'That's it Lieutenant Isambard! Get nice and close — have a good look at them!'

Podbury is back, carrying Isambard's chocolate ice-cream. He jogs eagerly up to Isambard, and gives him the ice-cream, and says, 'Wow! Look at that.'

I am looking at my beautiful husband, and my beautiful boy, as they look at the tigers, in the zoo, in London, in the sun. I am so warm. I am so grateful. I am so happy.

Why is Podbury holding a beer?

When he went to get Isambard's ice-cream he bought a beer for himself. He is drinking it. It is a pint of beer. He is drinking it fast.

This morning we were late to the zoo, because Podbury had been up the night before, playing poker with his friends. We are staying in a hotel in London for the week-end, and he has already drunk all the tiny bottles of vodka in our fridge. He spent last night at a casino.

On the way to the zoo, we had to stop for him to place a bet on a horse race. He bet nine thousand pounds. I know because I looked at the receipt.

When we arrived at the zoo, he heard on the radio that the horse he bet on had lost. I know because I saw his face.

He will be drunk tonight.

He will be drunk tomorrow. He was drunk yesterday, and the day before. Next week he leaves for Kenya, and for the first time I cannot go with him, because he will stand so close to the animals – just as he is standing so close to the tigers now.

He is standing by the railing, leaning on it, above the tigers. If I push him, he will fall in.

Why did he buy that beer?

We were happy, in the zoo, in the sun, and now he has bought a beer. He has bought a beer so he can get drunk, and go gambling.

Is he not happy enough with me and Isambard in the zoo? Is he not happy at all? I was so happy.

I am walking slowly toward him.

He is standing above the tigers.

I am reaching out my hand.

I am reaching out my hand towards Podbury's back, as he stands so close to the tigers.

If I were to push him, he would fall in.

Isambard is looking at me as I do this. He is silent. He stares at him. There is a strange look in his eyes. I do not know what he is thinking. What is he thinking?

What is Isambard thinking, as I reach out to push my husband into a pit of tigers?

* * *

Eugenia woke up screaming.

Her bed was soaked with sweat, and dust rose from her sheets as she sat up. A fly had been hiding under her pillow, and now it was awake too.

She was crying again. This was the first dream she'd had without those monsters in months. She wiped the sweat from her face and coughed, and cried, and shook. She had dreamed about her husband again.

Suddenly –

'ROOOOOOOAAAAARGGGHHH!!!!!'

Eugenia screamed once more.

It was almost more than she could bear. She leaped out of bed and ran to the window, shivering. From the barn, on the other side of the house, the noise came again.

'ROOOOOOOAAAAARGGGHHH!!!!!'

She squeaked and ran to put on her clothes. Hardly knowing what she was doing, she put on jeans, jumper, boots, coat, and stumbled out the door. She half-walked, half-fell down the stairs, sobbing as she went.

* * *

Hazel woke up in the dark, as blind as a bat.

It was cold. Was she in one of the rooms of the house? Was it night?

She seemed to be leaning upright against something,

but she didn't know what. She had no idea of where she was, or of the time.

Perhaps more disturbingly, there was, very definitely, something on her head. There was also, equally definitely, something on her face. Furthermore, the clothes she was wearing did not feel like her own. She tried to reach up to see what was on her head, but her hands were tied together – painfully tight.

All she could hear, at first, was her own breathing. Then other sounds revealed themselves – the owls, the wind in the trees, and somewhere, faintly, she was sure, the sound of someone else breathing. She wanted to look around to see where they were, but as her eyes adjusted she realised there was simply no light at all.

It felt as if she was wearing a costume.

She tried to be still, so as to pick out more sounds, but she was shaking and could not stop. How had she got herself into this mess?

She thought back to that first day of her arrival, when she was so disgusted by the rotting curtains, and filthy halls, and rude company. That day seemed like a picnic now.

She couldn't bring herself to try walking. Not knowing where she was, she had no idea what she might walk into it. She imagined, with dread, Geoff waiting in the darkness, jaws wide open.

'Hello?'

Hazel spun round, almost losing her balance. It was Eugenia's voice! But it was muffled – perhaps it was coming from behind a door.

'Hello? Who's there?'

Hazel, unexpectedly, was praying Eugenia would find her. Whatever Eugenia had done to Hazel, at least she wasn't a murderous lunatic like her son. If she found Hazel, it might all be OK.

Just as Hazel was about to call to her, she thought she heard the breathing again. There was *definitely* someone else in here with her. What if, as soon as she cried out, Geoff turned out to be right behind her and bit off her head?

Hazel tried not to cry. She'd promised herself she wouldn't cry any more in this house.

'Look here, answer me! Come out of there! This is private property!'

Whoever was in the dark with her said nothing, and so Hazel said nothing too.

'Well, I'm coming in there, and I expect an answer!'

Hazel was surprised by how far away the door was, as she heard Eugenia rattling it open.

'I know you're in there, whoever you are! I've heard some very loud noises coming from this barn!'

The barn – of course! That's why Hazel could hear the wind in the trees so clearly, and why the door was so far away. The barn was large – at least six times the size of the drawing room. Or at least that's what it looked like from the outside.

A ray of light shot in from the open door, and Hazel was blinded by it.

'I'm coming in!'

So in she came, carrying a walking stick, and waving it about wildly. Before she'd fired Boynce this would have been his job, and she didn't look like the sort of woman who spent much time patrolling her estates in the dead of night, ready to thrash intruders.

Hazel became more and more desperate to say something, but with each passing moment the breathing behind her became louder, and she became frightened of doing anything.

Eugenia, for her part, was becoming impatient.

'Look here, whoever you are, I'm fed up of this, and . . .'

Eugenia stopped. The light from the torch was directly in Hazel's eyes. She had seen her.

In an instant, Eugenia ran, full pelt, at Hazel. Before Hazel could cry out, she had shoved her hard in the chest with her walking stick.

She felt herself falling over the fence she had been propped up against, toppling onto the other side, and then, surprisingly, continuing to fall.

The ground on the other side of the fence was far below. Hazel yelped as she crashed into a bale of straw, spraying it up into the air as she landed. She promised herself that she wouldn't cry.

'Who are you? Tell me who you are or I'll thrash you to within an inch of your life! What are you after?! Do you want money?'

Eugenia was banging her walking stick on the fence, and Hazel could imagine if she was a burglar she would have run for her life long ago.

Then the noises started. Animal noises.

Hazel felt she was in some kind of pit – it was so deep, and the growling, squealing, grunting noises around her echoed off the walls.

If she'd managed to get Noel, Francis, and Geoff to make noises this scary when they were making nightmares she would have been very proud of them. They weren't amateurs now — this was the real thing. Palm-sweating, heart-beating, pant-wetting fear.

But Hazel knew that these were not the monsters she had befriended. Her friends would never have growled at her like that. They were Isambard's creations before they were her friends, and he had turned them on her.

'What on earth is that racket down there? What have you got down there, for heaven's sake? Are those animals I can hear?'

Eugenia wasn't letting herself be frightened.

Until someone turned on the lights.

There were long fluorescent lights at the top of the barn, and they lit up the place as clear as day. Hazel could see she was indeed in a pit. The monsters were emerging from under heaps of straw, snarling and spitting as they went. There was no way out — her hands were tied together, and the walls were far too steep to climb. She still refused to cry.

Eugenia was another matter. As Hazel saw her take in the scene, she saw every last shred of pride, snobbery, and arrogance dissolve. Eugenia's eyes were wide, and her mouth hung open. She looked like she'd seen a ghost.

'No . . . please . . . no. *Not again.*'

She was perfectly still, and had dropped her walking stick to the ground.

Somewhere in the barn, Hazel heard what she was certain was Isambard laughing — but Eugenia seemed deaf to it.

'I've done it again. *I've done it again.* My beautiful . . .'

It was then that Hazel realised what she was wearing. The thing on her face was a moustache. The thing on her head was a curly black wig. She was wearing a dark suit.

She was dressed as Podbury Pequierde.

This was Eugenia's worst nightmare.

'I'm sorry . . . I'm sorry . . . I didn't mean to – I swear! Oh! *Not again!*'

Hazel remembered how Sir Podbury Pequierde had died. One unfortunate summer's day, he had fallen into the tiger enclosure at London zoo. As Eugenia looked at Hazel, it was Podbury she was seeing. As she listened to the monsters, it was those tigers she was hearing. As she stood in the barn, it was the zoo she was remembering. Her husband had fallen to the tigers again, in front of her eyes.

Eugenia fell to the ground, clutching her chest. She was finding it hard to breathe. She gasped like a fish out of water. Still she could not take her eyes away from what she saw. Was she having a heart attack?

Somewhere in the barn, Isambard laughed.

Hazel knew then that the monsters would eat her alive if Isambard told them to – why wouldn't they? They were monsters, after all. She would be the living recreation of Podbury's death.

Now she started crying.

'Help!' she squeaked, pathetically.

Eugenia seemed to hear her.

Realisation dawned on her face, and her breathing slowed.

'. . . Hazel?! Hazel! Oh my, Hazel, it's you down there! Wait – wait there, my girl, I'll . . . I'll . . .'

Eugenia shook her head. She seemed to be snapping out of her shock.

Isambard stopped laughing.

'Wait there, I'll find some rope!'

Eugenia stumbled off, out of sight from where Hazel was.

The monsters stopped making noises.

As Hazel looked over to her left, she could see Francis, his head still half-buried in straw. He was staring at where Eugenia had been, stunned. As she looked over to the right, little Noel was the same. It was like they didn't understand what she was doing – as if this wasn't part of the plan.

'What's she doing?' asked Noel softly.

'I THINK SHE'S — TRYING TO SAVE HER?'

Eugenia had found what she was looking for.

'Wait there! I'm coming! I'm coming!'

A long, dusty old rope cascaded down into the pit.

'My dear, I know you're frightened, but I need you to take hold of the rope! Can you do that?'

Hazel had *never* been spoken to by Eugenia like this before.

'Yeah! OK, I'll try!'

They hadn't just recreated Podbury's death – they'd given Eugenia the chance to make it different this time. This time she could save her husband rather than watching him die.

The monsters – Geoff included, as he had now come

out from the back of the pit — had clearly been expecting her to drop dead with fright.

The idea had been to literally frighten her to death — but it had backfired.

That was when Isambard called the whole thing off. He ran out from the bale of straw he'd been hiding behind.

'Stop it! Stop it! That's all wrong! That's not what happened! That's not what you did!'

He was on the other side of the pit to Eugenia, screaming, and crying, and jumping up and down. His face was bright red, and his eyes seemed bright red too. He was wearing his black suit, and black bow tie, and his black hair looked just like the wig that Hazel was wearing. It was hard to believe someone so small could contain so much anger.

'You didn't save him! Did you? *Did you?* You didn't throw a rope in! Because you killed him! You wanted him to die!'

Eugenia, having seemed together when she was throwing the rope down, fell apart again. Her quiet, shy son, was the master of her nightmare.

'What are you doing here? What's going on? Please, Isambard, darling, you don't know what you're talking about . . .'

'I do! You pushed him! You hated him and you wanted him to die! YOU KILLED HIM!'

'It wasn't like that . . . I . . . I didn't mean to . . . I didn't know what I was doing . . . I loved him . . .'

But it was too much for her. She sat down on the ground, and stopped talking. She looked like a little girl, younger than Hazel, and very ashamed of herself. She was too sad to cry. Her son had done all this – dug the pit, made the monsters, kidnapped Hazel – all to frighten his own mother to death.

Hazel looked at the monsters, who still held their eyes on Eugenia. They didn't seem to know what to make of it. This was, Hazel guessed, not the kind of murderer that Isambard had told them about – told them to hate and to kill. She was just a sad, broken woman, racked with guilt and remorse. The monsters stood still.

'Geoff! Noel! Francis! Kill her! Kill her! Tear her to shreds!'

Geoff did not move. He just looked at Eugenia. Then his low, leopard voice rumbled out from the pit.

'That wasn't the plan, Isambard.'

Isambard howled.

'The plan's changed! It's changed! Kill her! *Kill her!*'

Geoff looked as if he was having feelings a leopard had never had before. He stood there, unable to move. Then, slowly, he turned.

'What are you doing! Why are you just standing there! *Kill her!*'

Geoff took a deep breath.

'She threw the girl a rope, Isambard. She threw her a rope.'

'She killed my *father!*'

Isambard was beside himself.

'Do it!'

Geoff held his gaze.

'No.'

Isambard screamed.

Out from behind him, without warning, he produced a shotgun.

It was almost too big for him to lift. No shotgun is made for a ten-year-old to use. But he held it out in front of him, aiming it at Eugenia's head.

Then, suddenly knowing for certain that they had been doing the bidding of a madman, the monsters then did something they had never thought they would do. They turned on their creator.

Noel scurried swiftly up the side of the pit, Geoff climbed up the rocky walls with his powerful gorilla arms, and Francis leapt out in a single bound. They stood in between Isambard and his mother, growling.

'What are you doing! Get out of my way! Let me kill her!'

Isambard was having to wipe the tears out of his eyes to see.

'Get out of my way – *please!*'

Then he fired a shot into the air. It was enough to knock him onto the ground, and wind him severely.

The monsters didn't even flinch. As they began to move forward towards him, he ran, clutching his side. He blubbered and sobbed as he rushed away from where Hazel could see. She could hear the monsters snarling as they chased after him.

Hazel looked about, amazed to be alive. The pit was empty but for her.

Isambard had fled, his own monsters in hot pursuit.

Eugenia sat at the top of the pit, perfectly still.

Now that she could see what she was doing, Hazel wriggled free of the wire binding her hands, got to her feet, and checked to see if she was hurt. She seemed to be all right, and what's more, the rope was still hanging down into the pit. She took off the moustache and the wig, and tested to see if the rope was secure. Eugenia must have tied it around something.

With a bit of effort (but what was a bit more effort after what had happened tonight?) Hazel clambered out, to stand panting at the edge of the pit, Eugenia beside her.

Again, Hazel was struck by how young she looked. She took off Podbury's jacket, and threw it around her shoulders.

'Come on, Aunt Eugenia. We should get back inside.'

Eugenia grabbed her arm, and looked her in the eyes.

'I did mean to.'

Hazel didn't think she was the best person for Eugenia to talk to about this.

'I did mean to. I wanted to kill him. I went to push him . . .'

'Why?' – if it came to this, Hazel at least wanted to know why her Aunt had murdered her uncle.

Eugenia started to cry.

Hazel sat down beside her, very tired.

'Because he drank.' She sniffed. 'Because he gambled. That's all. He was spending everything we had, and it was ruining our lives, and . . . and . . . I didn't understand why he couldn't be happy with us without drinking. I . . . I . . .' She began to cry again and said no more.

They sat there, aunt and niece, under the harsh fluorescent glow of the barn. The owls were silent now, though the wind was still screaming in the trees.

Hazel's last surprise of the night was when she put her arm around Eugenia, and, just as she imagined her mother would, hugged her.

Eugenia hugged her back, and buried her face in the hair of her ten-year-old niece.

'But I changed my mind.'

Hazel sighed.

'Don't lie, auntie.'

Eugenia sobbed harder.

'No! Really! I marched over there, and I was so angry, and I just knew that he'd bet thousands of pounds on the horses that day already, and I knew when we left the zoo he'd leave me and Isambard at home to go play poker with his friends, and I wanted so much to have him out of my life, and . . . and I went to push him, but . . . but I changed my mind.'

Hazel stroked her aunt's face.

'So how come he ended up in the tiger enclosure?'

Eugenia was crying so hard Hazel worried she might burst. She held Hazel tightly, and clutched her hair in her hands.

'I tripped!'

After that, Eugenia was lost to the world.

Hazel knew that she had told the truth. Holding her gently, in the cold, windy barn, she just knew it was perfectly true. Like Hazel, like Geoff, like Noel, like Francis, Eugenia had changed her mind. Just before doing something awful, she had changed her mind.

She'd meant to do it. She had done it. But it was still an accident. At the moment of murder, Podbury's death was not what Eugenia had wanted.

Over the sound of the wind, far away, the ducks quacked forlornly on the lake. The pigs must have been in their pen too, curled up on piles of straw. And Bullivant would be outside his kennel. He had stood guard outside it every night since Hazel had arrived, loyally protecting the home of the noble family Pequierde. Every night he stood out there, listening for intruders he could not hear, watching a house he could not see, waiting for a master who would never come.

Epilogue

So what do you think?

Who was bad? Who was worst? Was anybody good?

Isambard was trying to avenge the murder of his father. Hazel was trying to rebel against a tyrannical aunt. Eugenia had not truly meant to kill her husband – and she was only as cruel as she was because of the way the grief and remorse tormented her. Surely these three fine human beings qualify as goodies?

No?

Well, I suppose you're right. It's really a story of villains. A woman murdering her husband and bullying everyone around her. A boy trying to kill his mother. A girl torturing her aunt with invention and cruelty beyond her years. The creatures in the forest were not the only monsters in this story.

What's that you say? They had reasons? But everyone has reasons. Everyone has reasons for everything.

Isambard had vanished. Geoff, Noel and Francis looked over every inch of the forest, but he had escaped them that stormy night and was now long gone.

In the two days left before her parents collected her, Hazel saw the wounds of the house begin to heal. Eugenia admitted she had been wrong to fire Dungeon, Pude and Boynce, and, with a mumbled set of apologies the like of which no one ever thought they would see, she offered them their jobs back. They accepted, on the condition that Eugenia treat them better. She promised she would.

The monsters did not venture into the house again, but it was understood that they no longer planned to kill Eugenia. They seemed ashamed, if that was something a monster could be. Hazel, having been frightened that they were going to eat her alive, found that she began to miss them, though it didn't yet feel right to go and talk to them.

Hazel and Eugenia ate lunch together and even managed to play a card game or two afterwards. With Isambard gone, they took it in turns to feed his pets. Getting the purée into Bullivant's tube took some getting used to, but the pigs seemed very excited about all the gravy Mrs Dungeon had started feeding them. It was decided that the ducks should be weened off their cigarettes. A box of nicotine patches was bought, and the difficult business of catching them and sticking the patches under their feathers was begun.

Mrs Dungeon was delighted to find a quiet, polite bell had been installed for when Eugenia wanted tea, and when it was brought to her she had begun to say, sincerely, 'Thank you, Mrs Dungeon.' Sleeping eight hours a night was doing wonders for Eugenia's mood. The first night she managed twelve and awoke with a blissful smile on her face.

On the final day, a couple of hours before Dougal and Katie arrived, Eugenia sat Hazel down in the drawing room.

The curtains had been drawn. The mushrooms had been cleaned off the sofa (by Eugenia) and the piles of magazines tidied away. It wasn't what you would call clean, but it was a start.

'Now, before your parents come to pick you up, I wanted to have a little word with you, Peanut . . .'

' . . . Hazel.'

'Yes! Sorry – Hazel. Um . . . yes, I just wanted to say – thank you.'

They both smiled. This was not an easy thing for a woman as proud as Eugenia to say.

'You've . . . well . . . thank you. The other thing I wanted to say was that I'd rather you didn't tell your parents that Isambard is missing.'

She seemed to be preparing herself to do something very difficult.

'It's my responsbility, and I want to do it on my own.'

Hazel frowned.

'Do what on your own?'

Eugenia sipped at her tea.

'Make peace with my son. I need to find him on my own, and make my apology on my own, and . . . win him back on my own.'

Hazel nodded.

'How are you going to find him.'

'I don't know. But I'll find a way. I'm sure he's out there. Out there somewhere.'

Hazel realised that there had once been three people in this family, and now there was only one. There would never be three again – but maybe there could be two.

With that, Eugenia drifted off into her private thoughts again, and Hazel decided to leave her in peace.

She took an hour to tidy up her things and say goodbye to Mrs Dungeon – who gave her a little flask of gravy for the journey – and then waited quietly in the hall.

With only half an hour to go, Boynce knocked on the window. She opened the door for him.

'Hello, dear. You all right?'

'Yeah, fine thanks.'

'Mmm. Sad to be going?'

She laughed.

'A bit maybe.'

He smiled warmly, and tousled her hair.

'I've a message for you miss.'

'A message.'

'Yup. From your friends in the woods. They say if you write a letter to me, I'll pass it on to them – which I will – and they'll be sure to write you back.'

Boynce winked slyly at her. Then he gave her a peck on the cheek, and wandered off.

An hour later, Hazel was in the car, speeding away from that collapsing old house, surrounded by chocolates, and very happy to be back with Mum and Dad.

This was the hard bit.

'Mum?'

'Oh, Hazel, please, I'm so jet-lagged, and if you say anything horrible about my sister I won't be able to bear it . . .'

'No! I wasn't . . . I mean . . .'

Hazel sighed. She had never thought she would say this.

'It was fine . . . in the end . . . we . . . sort of became friends.'

Hazel's mother Katie turned round, baffled.

'Well . . . I suppose that's good news.'

Then she smiled.

'Oh, Hazel, I'm so glad! You see! She's all right once you get to know her.'

* * *

It is not easy to be friends. Even if the people you're trying to make friends with aren't frogstriches, or gorilleopards, or pythupines, or murderers or lunatics. People are difficult, and lonely, and angry, and that's all there is to it.

But you should have a go anyway. However frightening people are, you should definitely try to get to know them.

Because nobody likes a scaredy-cat.

Off to bed now.